A SAVAGE DOPEBOY 2

Ghost

Lock Down Publications and Ca$h
Presents
A Savage Dopeboy 2
A Novel by *Ghost*

Lock Down Publications
P.O. Box 870494
Mesquite, Tx 75187

Visit our website @
www.lockdownpublications.com

Lock Down Publications
Like our page on Facebook: Lock Down Publications @
www.facebook.com/lockdownpublications.ldp
Cover design and layout by: **Dynasty Cover Me**
Book interior design by: **Shawn Walker**
Edited by: **Kiera Northington**

Stay Connected with Us!

Text **LOCKDOWN** to 22828 to stay up-to-date with new releases, sneak peaks, contests and more…
Thank you.

Submission Guideline.

Submit the first three chapters of your completed manuscript to ldpsubmissions@gmail.com, subject line: Your book's title. The manuscript must be in a .doc file and sent as an attachment. Document should be in Times New Roman, double spaced and in size 12 font. Also, provide your synopsis and full contact information. If sending multiple submissions, they must each be in a separate email.

Have a story but no way to send it electronically? You can still submit to LDP/Ca$h Presents. Send in the first three chapters, written or typed, of your completed manuscript to:

LDP: Submissions Dept
Po Box 870494
Mesquite, Tx 75187

DO NOT send original manuscript. Must be a duplicate.

Provide your synopsis and a cover letter containing your full contact information.

Only if your submission is **approved**, will you then get a response letter.

Thanks for considering LDP and Ca$h Presents.

Dedications:

First of all, this book is dedicated to my Baby Girl 3/10, the love of my life and purpose for everything I do. As long as I'm alive, you'll never want nor NEED for anything. We done went from flipping birds to flipping books. The best is yet to come.

To LDP'S CEO- Ca$h & COO- Shawn:

I would like to thank y'all for this opportunity. The wisdom, motivation, and encouragement that I've received from you two is greatly appreciated.

The grind is real. The loyalty in this family is real. I'm riding with LDP 'til the wheels fall off.

THE GAME IS OURS!

Ghost

Chapter 1

Jahrome couldn't believe he'd just seen his mother laid out on a slab in the morgue. Her body beaten, mangled and desecrated in every single way. He sat back in his seat with a heavy heart, as a tear slid down his cheek and dripped off his chin. He held his sister, Babygirl, firmer in his arms as she rocked back and forth in the back seat, sobbing against him.

"Why are we going through all of these things? Why would they do that to our mother? She was so nice. She would never hurt nobody. It just isn't fair," she said, before sticking her face nearly under his arm and breaking down worse than before.

Mami sat in the front seat scrolling down her call log, looking for her uncle's number. She was tired of Atlanta, tired of all the drama that came along with it. In one week, she had lost her brother to murder, right along with her niece's mother. Both of their heads blown off their bodies. It had broken her heart to hear about him. Then, her three cousins had also been caught in the gunmen's crossfire. Five lives lost, and all for what? She felt sick to her stomach and was ready for a change.

She knew her uncle would accept her, her man Jahrome, and his sister Babygirl with open arms, and give them the protection they would need. He was a savage, knee-deep in the game, and he loved her. As soon as she found his number, she clicked on it and listened to it ring a few times, before going to voicemail. She sent him a quick text, letting him know she was headed down to Savannah to visit, had a couple people with her, and she needed his help. She turned around in her seat to let Jahrome know where they were headed. "Papi, I just called texted my uncle and let him know that we're on our way down there, so I think we should go get a few of our things, and then leave this place behind. There is too much shit happening around here. Before you know it, I feel like something is going to happen to one of us, and I wouldn't be able to take that." She blinked and shook her head, just imagining the worst possible scenarios, before turning around and starting her truck and putting it in drive.

Jahrome leaned down and kissed his sister on the forehead because she was shaking underneath him. "I'm ready to bounce too, baby. If you feeling your people a let us chill until I can get shit situated, then let's go that route. But I'm letting you know now, we ain't finna be there for long and as soon as I get my head straight, I'm fucking that nigga Jock over, because I know he the only one that put this hit on my mother, that's if he ain't do the shit himself." Jahrome had killed Reggie, Jock's little brother. Jock was a major nigga out of Bankhead who was a real street nigga and about that life. His name was crazy in the slums, and everything about it said he wasn't the nigga to be fucked with. Jahrome had killed Reggie after he found him beating Babygirl nearly to death, before leaving a long gash across her face. He beat the nigga senseless and dumped his body in the river, and in his opinion that's where it belonged.

Mami nodded her head while putting the car in drive, with her foot on the brake. "Papi, I already know how you get down. I just want you to holla at him first, then once we chill for a minute and he set you up, I'll support whatever decision you make, because you're my man and I love you. I'm riding wit you no matter what. Ride or die. I mean that shit," she said as the rain started to fall heavily from the sky, the thunder roaring like an angry lion.

Jahrome held Babygirl firmer in his arms as something told him to look up. He just got that feeling deep within the pit of his gut. It was as if the whole world slowed down at a snail's pace. An all-black Navigator sped down the street swiftly and then slammed on its brakes right beside their truck. *Vroooom!* *Errr-uh!* He saw the men jump out with black masks over their faces and assault rifles and that's when the gunfire started.

Boom-boom-boom-boom-boom-boom-boom-boom! *Boo-wa!* *Boo-wa!* *Boo-wa!* *Boo-wa!*

Their truck windows shattered, and the truck rocked from side to side. Babygirl screamed at the top of her lungs, and Jahrome threw his body on top of hers as the truck's interior looked like it was being torn to shreds. And then there was Mami's screams, so loud they pierced his ears.

Boom-boom-boom boom-boom-boom-boom-boom-boom! Boom!

"Get the fuck out of here!" he hollered up at her, before taking his .40 Glock from the small of his back and bussing outward toward the shooters. He couldn't make out where they were, he just saw they were shooting from somewhere in the middle of the street against their Navigator. Had they run all the way up to their truck, they would have been able to finish the three off. The rain came down harder and Mami ducked down and slammed on the gas, as lightning flashed across the sky. Her tires burned rubber skirting away from the curb, smoke coming from under them and she drove in a panic, constantly checking her rear-view mirrors. The men ran back to the Navigator, jumped in and seemed to be making a U-turn, before coming in their direction. Mami stepped on the gas and flew through the red light. A car that had the right of way blew its horn loudly, before slamming into the back of her truck's bumper, and knocking the truck off course somewhat. The truck swerved, winding up on the curb, releasing the airbag. Mami bumped her head on the steering wheel. She was already having a hard time seeing through the caved in windshield. She shook her head, leaning to the side to try and see out of the windshield so she could make her escape.

Jahrome saw the Navigator come through the intersection and before they could get within fifty yards of them, he leaned his head out the window with the .40 Glock in his hand, aiming directly at the driver through their own windshield.

Boom! Boom! Boom! Boom! Boom! Boom!

"Baby, get the fuck out of here!" he yelled as he watched the Navigator swerve and crash into a parked car. "Bitch ass niggas!"

Mami took her pocketknife and stabbed the air bag. It exploded and she pushed it back into the steering wheel, before stepping on the gas and driving the truck on the sidewalk, all the way until she got to the end of the block. She made a right, then another left, before taking a long alley, that led onto a one-way street. As soon as she turned onto the street, the truck died. It just simply cut off and started rolling for about twenty yards. "Fuck! Fuck! Fuck! This can't be happening right now. Not right now! Damn you!" she screamed, slammed both of her hands on the steering wheel with tears rolling down her cheeks.

The rain picked up so hard that they could barely see the street they were on. Lightning flashed across the sky, before there was a loud boom. Jahrome stuck his head out the window and saw the Navigator was at the beginning of the alley about a block down. His heart beat fast in his chest. He was ready to die than to allow anything to happen to his sister or his woman. "Look, y'all get up out this truck, jump that fence and hide under that porch right there. Don't come from under that ma'fucka until I tell you to, you understand me?" he hollered, watching the Navigator get closer.

"No! I'm not leaving you! I need you, Jahrome!" Babygirl yelled and wrapped her arms around him. He pulled them off of him.

"Babygirl, get yo ass out this car, sis, or we finna die. Now, I gotta handle these niggas. Please, just listen to me. I'm begging you." He leaned over and opened the door on the other side. "Now go!"

Mami wanted to climb into the backseat and wrap her arms around him as well, but she knew it would have been ill-advised. So instead, she jumped out of her driver's seat and pulled Babygirl from the truck. "Come on, girl. Let him handle his business. He know what he doing. Be careful, Papi, and know that I love you!" she hollered, pulling Babygirl by the hand. The rain picked up speed, and now it felt like they were being attacked by grains of rice. Babygirl looked over her shoulder at her brother, as he ran for a few feet and crouched down on the side of a house. She wanted to go with him. She wanted to be by his side. If something was going to happen to them, then she wanted to be in his arms when it did. He was all that mattered in life. The further she got away from him, the more it hurt her heart. The thunder roared in the sky, then there was a loud boom and a tree fell in front of her and Mami, causing both girls to scream at the top of their lungs. The tree fell onto somebody's porch, luckily not the one Jahrome had told them to hide under. They double-timed and made it three houses down, before hustling and climbing under the white house's porch he had pointed out.

Jahrome curled his lip and held his .40 Glock tighter in his hand. He saw the Navigator stop and then the doors opened, with two of the masked men getting out of it with the assault rifles in their hands. He took a deep breath and watched them for a second longer. He was crouched down on the side of a house, and they had stopped in the alley, directly behind the same house. He took another deep breath and slowly made his way toward the truck, thanking God it had gotten extremely dark out. The wind picked up and the rain was coming down aggressively. He could barely move without feeling like he was being weighed down. His clothes were matted to him and he felt like he was about to pass out from being in a state of hysteria. Before he could make it all the way to the Navigator, he heard feet crunching on grass, and then somebody coughing. He looked into the next yard and saw one of the masked men walking carefully through the backyard right next to the one he was in, as if he was worried about stepping on a landmine or something.

Jahrome couldn't believe his luck. He looked around to make sure the other gunman was nowhere in sight. Unable to locate him, he nodded his head and decided to run back around the front of the house and post up at the exit point of the gangway the masked man was coming out of, just as the thunder roared overhead. He crouched down and got as close to the porch as possible, and as soon as the masked gunman got about ten feet away from him, he fell on his back and aimed toward his head.

Boom! Boom! Boom!

The masked man jumped backward and fell to a knee, holding his throat. He looked like he was choking. Jahrome hopped up and ran toward him, aiming for his head.

Boom! Boom! Boom! Click! Click! Click!

Fuck, he was out of bullets. The masked gunman fell on his side, his body shaking and bleeding out after receiving multiple gunshots to his face and neck. Jahrome ran over and picked up his SK, he noted it had a thirty-round magazine. He was thankful for that and also severely paranoid.

He ducked back down and looked around for the other shooter he'd seen get out of the truck. He tried his best to listen for shoes on wet grass but heard nothing of the like. Finally, he rose and made his way back toward the truck, still parked in the alley with its lights on. He picked up speed and before he got into the alley, he ducked down on the side of the garage and took a deep breath, then shot into the alley, running directly at the driver's window.

Boom-boom-boom! Boom-boom-boom!

The driver's side window shattered before turning red, and the horn blew loudly. The back door of the truck opened, and another shooter made his way out of it. Jahrome dropped to the ground and chopped at his legs.

"Arrrgh! Muthafucka!" the masked gunman hollered out, just as the lightning flashed through the sky behind him. He fell to his knees and held down the trigger to the assault rifle.

Boom-boom-boom!

Fire spit from the barrel of his gun, illuminating the night's sky. Jahrome closed one of his eyes, aiming directly at the man, and pulled the trigger.

Boom-boom-boom! Boom-boom-boom!

The bullets ate away the gunman's face and knocked him backward about five feet.

Boom! Boom! Boom!

Bullets slammed into the body of the truck right by Jahrome's head, knocking sparks from the truck. Before he could think of anything else to do, he rolled under the truck as more shots rang out in the night. "Fuck is this bitch nigga? Where is he bussing from?" he asked himself out loud, with sweat and rain pouring down his forehead. He thought about his sister and woman and prayed they were okay. He would never allow anything to happen to them, he vowed that on his life.

Boom! *Boom*! *Boom*!

Bullets slammed into the concrete right by him on his left side. It made the hairs stand up along his arms. Way off in the distance police sirens were blaring in the night. He didn't know if they were headed in his direction or not, but what he did know was that he had to get out of that situation and fast. He heard sneakers on the wet concrete along with the rain, before they stopped. He peeked from under the truck and saw another gunman laying down on his stomach, getting ready to aim his weapon at him, but before he could fire, he rolled from under the truck.

Boom-boom-boom! *Boom-boom-boom*!

One of the bullets slammed into one of the back tires. There was a loud buzzing sound, before the truck looked lopsided. Jahrome jumped up letting off three rounds at the gunman.

Boom! *Boom*! *Boom*!

Then he ran on the side of the garage before throwing down the AK and yelling, "Fuck, I'm out of bullets! " He knelt down right at the opening of the gangway, praying that the gunman took the bait and tried to run behind him. He pulled out the nine-millimeter from his waist and cocked it back, laying on his back, ready to fire.

Lightning flashed across the sky and then there was the rumbling of thunder. The rain beat down against his face as he swallowed repeatedly and held his breath, until he became light-headed. He waited for what seemed like a whole hour, though only a few minutes had passed, before he heard the truck start up and storm down the alley, just as the police sirens got louder. He jumped up from the ground and ran along the side of the house, across the street and to the porch his girls were hiding under. As soon as they saw him, they both screamed at the same time. Mami felt like she was about to have a heart attack, and Babygirl could barely breathe. She was afraid to look him over closely from fear he had been shot somewhere. He extended his hands to them. "Come on y'all, we gotta get the fuck out of here."

Ghost

Chapter 2

Dymond allowed the tears to flow down her cheeks, as she wrapped her hands tighter around her nine-year-old daughter's neck and squeezed with all of her might. The little girl kicked her little legs and tried to break free, to no avail. Her eyes got bigger and bigger until the life slowly left her body. Her last thoughts were of missing her daddy and wishing he was there to protect her from her evil mommy. Dymond choked harder and harder, before letting her daughter's neck go and looking down on her lifeless body. She rocked back and forth on her knees in disbelief. "What have I done? What have I done?" she whimpered, before standing up with both of her hands against her face. Aerial laid on her back with her eyes wide open, unseeing. Her caramel face now blue, her little tongue halfway out of her mouth. Dymond could still see her finger marks around the little girl's neck.

"I didn't want to do that, baby. I swear I didn't. Mommy didn't want to kill you, but I need to be happy. I need to be free, and you were going to tell your daddy on me. Please forgive me. I'll see you in heaven, I promise," she said, rushing to the last open safe and stuffing Jock's bricks of heroin and cocaine inside of a designer bag. She knew she had to get away from Jock. She had to get away from him before he or somebody killed her, just to get back at him. After she finished loading up the dope, she took the other designer bags she had filled up with his money and zipped them up, before kneeling down and calling Big Gunz's phone. Big Gunzs, who she often referred to as Gunz, was Jock's right-hand man, and the person she was set to run away to Miami with. They had already planned everything out. Gunz had always been there for here emotionally. He had always been that shoulder she needed when Jock knocked her so far into the ground that she felt trapped. She felt Gunz was her rescuer. He would be the man to break the mold in her life, so she would do anything for him, including kill her own daughter because she felt like neither Aerial, nor Jock gave a fuck about her anyway. She was at a point in her life where she wanted to be happy, and both of them stood in the way of that.

Gunz picked up his phone on the first ring and she damn near bit her tongue, trying to get her words out. "Baby, I got everything and I'm ready to go right now. Meet me on Franklin Place in twenty minutes."

He told her, "I'll be there," before hanging up the phone. Dymond ran around like a chicken with their head cut off, before she finally finished loading up her Benz truck. As soon as she closed the door, the rain started to come down heavily and she saw Jock rolling down the street before pulling into their driveway, right alongside her truck. She felt like she wanted to shit on herself.

* * *

Jock frowned as he pulled into his driveway. He had a headache that was killing him so bad that he'd forgotten to snatch up the Haitians' hundred and twenty-five thousand dollars that he owed them for the week. The last thing he needed was to be going to war over some chump change. When he saw his baby mother getting into the Benz truck that he'd bought her for her last birthday, he found that a little odd and it irritated him, especially because before he'd left less than fifteen minutes ago, he told her to clean up his fucking house. The fact that she was set to leave was pissing him off and he felt like he needed to get to the bottom of it. He pulled alongside her truck and lowered his window, just as she did the same. The rain splashed into the truck and further infuriated him. He felt like getting out and kicking her ass. She was lucky his head hurt as bad as it did, because if it didn't, he would have fucked her up just for the sport of it. To him, there was nothing like whooping a woman's ass and putting her in her place. It just made him feel stronger. He looked into her pretty face and mugged the shit out of her. "Where the fuck you finna go?" he asked with venom. Dymond passed gas and started to shake in her seat. *Father, please just let me make it out of this driveway. I'm sorry for killing my daughter, but you know that I had to.* She took a deep breath.

"Baby, I gotta go get some bleach and Ajax. I want that house to be spic and span. I don't want you whooping my ass. Ain't nobody got time for that," she said, trying to make a small joke that landed flat. Jock curled his upper lip. His dark-skinned handsome face frowned into a mask of anger.

"Bitch, you mean to tell me you ain't got all of that shit already? What the fuck you be in there doing all day? You ain't got no job." He shook his head in disgust and annoyance. Dymond swallowed and bit into her bottom lip. She could feel the sweat rolling down her back. Her underarms were moist, sweat ran from under her breasts and dripped into her bra, making her really uncomfortable.

"Yeah, I know I should have been paying more attention, but I'm sorry. I'll try and do better from here on out. I promise," she whimpered. Jock hated when she started to cry. It irritated him more than anything in the world. The worst thing to him was a whiny female. He hated it.

"You know what, get yo ass in the house. I'm finna fuck you up, and I bet you don't forget to get none of that shit again." He turned off his ignition, took his keys and entered into the rain, jogging to the house and nearly slipping on the wet concrete. As soon as he got on the porch, he looked back into the driveway and waited for Dymond to get out of the truck, and his eyes got as big as saucers when he saw what she did. Dymond threw the truck in reverse and stormed out of the driveway and into the street, slamming on the brakes. She rolled down her passenger's window and looked at him as he stood on the porch looking dumbfounded.

"I hate you, Jock! I mean, I hate yo guts! Have a nice life!" She stepped on the gas and stormed down the street, before coming to a stop at the end of the block. He saw her brake lights come on, and then she made a left and skirted down to the next block. He ran out into the rain and got into his truck, ready to chase her, but then his money came to mind.

"Fuck!" He slammed his truck door and ran into the house, slipping on the steps before regaining his balance and running inside and straight up the stairs. "I know this bitch didn't! I know this bitch didn't! This punk ass bitch!" he hollered again and again, until he made it into his bedroom and saw it had been ransacked. It looked like a tornado had hit it. Then he saw his daughter in the middle of the floor with her eyes wide open, along with her mouth. Her tongue rested along her jaw, her face a bluish color. His heart felt like it split down the middle. He fell to his knees as the tears ran down his cheeks. His throat felt like it was swollen, he felt dizzy and sick. He crawled to her slowly and picked her up into his arms. Her body was still warm, though heavier than what he was used to her being.

"Baby, wake up. Baby, wake up. Daddy don't feel like playing right now," he said out loud, with his voice breaking up. Tears ran down his face as he cried harder. He kissed her on the forehead and placed his hand over her heart. There was no heartbeat. She continued to look toward the ceiling with unseeing eyes. Her neck hung backward on her shoulders, a slight scent of death emanating from her body. He rocked with her in his arms. "Baby, I need you. Please wake up, Princess.

I need you. Don't die on me. Daddy need you, because you the only one that matter. I need my little girl. Please," he groaned, with snot running out of his nose. He held his daughter tight, shaking his head in disbelief, rocking back and forth for an entire hour before he had enough courage to lower her back to the floor.

The whole time, thoughts of betrayal ran through his mind. He couldn't believe Dymond would do such a thing, that she would kill her own daughter. He knew she was jealous of her, but he never knew how much. He felt like killing her entire family and he knew he probably would, with no mercy. His daughter was his everything, she was his pride and joy. With her laying lifeless at his feet, the world became a darker place. He slowly got up and looked around the room. He looked toward the closet and had already guessed his safe had been opened and emptied, but he still walked over there to confirm it. At seeing the proof, he fell to his knees and shook his head. Nearly a million dollars, gone. He slowly made his way to her closet and saw the same result, his safe opened and emptied. All of his dope gone. All of the Haitians' fronted dope, gone. He fell to his knees with his hands over his ears, shaking his head. He felt like he was going crazy.

* * *

Dymond got to Franklin Street and pulled behind Gunz's black BMW Sport. Before jumping out into the rain, he met her halfway and picked her up into his arms. She wrapped her legs around him and started to kiss all over his lips. "I told you, baby," she said, between more kissing and sucking. "I told you I would do anything for you. I got everything. I got all of the money and all of the dope. I'm ready to go. Please, let's get out of here," she groaned.

Gunz put her down and told her to get into the front seat of his whip, while he grabbed all of the bags of money and dope. He felt giddy, like he had hit a major lick and he had. As soon as all of the stuff was loaded into his car, he lost all loyalty and respect for Jock. He just no longer cared about him. The only thing that mattered was Dymond, and the money and dope that came along with her.

* * *

Jock had received another text from the Haitians, asking where he was, but he failed to respond. He didn't know what to tell them, or what to do. He sat in the middle of his bedroom holding his dead daughter, crying real tears, shaking his head in anger. He promised to make a whole lot of muthafuckas pay for her death. Anybody he thought was related to Dymond was about to get it. And at the same time, he would have to get revenge for his brother's murder and deal wit the Haitians, because they were sure to come at him hard soon if he didn't respond in regard to their money. He hit Gunz's cell again, praying that he picked up so they could fuck Atlanta over.

Chapter 3

"Girl, what the fuck? Get y'all ass in here," Berto said, stepping to the side so his cousin Mami, Jahrome, and Babygirl could step into the house, before he closed the door behind them. Berto peeked out the window with two pistols in his hands and curled his upper lip. He didn't know if anybody had followed them, but he'd heard about what had taken place with Rico, and he didn't want that drama on his father's doorstep. However, if it came, he promised to be more than ready for it. Mami stepped into the living room and ran her arms up and down her shoulders. She was freezing cold and shaking like a leaf. She looked her cousin up and down before shaking her head, eyeing the pistols.

"What the fuck you got those out for? Don't tell me it's more bullshit going on down here in Savannah, because I'm so tired of it." She paced back and forth, trying to peel her wet clothes away from her, walking to the thermostat and turning the heat up. Babygirl walked into Jahrome's arms, and he wrapped them around her. He could feel her shaking like crazy. It made him want to throw a blanket around her.

"Say bro, you got a blanket or something they can wrap up in?"

Berto nodded and looked back to Mami. "Fuck, Mami, you haven't been here for five minutes before you're chewing me out." He walked past her and into the long hallway that led to the master bedroom. The whole house looked to be covered in crucifixes. A person could glean that the family staying there were devout Catholics.

"I'm not chewing you out, Berto. I just wanna make sure there isn't a bunch of bullshit going on here like it is back in Atlanta. Do you know I haven't even buried Rico yet, and it feels like his enemies are already trying to kill us too?" she said, a little louder than normal to make sure he could hear her at the back of the house. Berto put both of his guns back into their holsters and grabbed two blankets out of the linen closet, before closing the door back. He loved his cousins, always had. They had grown up together in Clayton County. His father and their mother were siblings. For as long as he could remember, his cousin Mami always got on his ass about everything, which pissed him off because she was only two years older than him. He came back into the living room and sat the blankets on the couch, looking over at Jahrome and Babygirl.

Jahrome grabbed one of the blankets right away, unfolding it and wrapping it around Babygirl's shoulders. She shook the whole time and it made him feel some type of way. "Wrap this around you, sis, before you get sick." He looked over at Mami. "You get over here too." Mami felt a little jealous that he had tended to his sister first. She felt like since he was her man, she should have been first on his list of priorities. But instead of arguing with him or showing her displeasure, she simply made her way over to him and allowed him to place her within the blanket. Babygirl couldn't take her eyes off of Berto. She had never seen a man so fine in all of her life. His golden skin and handsome face with the bright blue eyes, were driving her crazy. She had never seen hair so curly and silky. She was trying her best to find a flaw on him, but she could not. He wore a wife beater and his arms were ripped, the white shirt showcased the ripples of his stomach muscles and he even smelled good. She had to shake her head to get out of the zone, because he had that kind of an effect on her.

Berto pulled Mami by the arm into the kitchen was located at the back of the downstairs landing. Once there, he hugged her and looked into her brown eyes. "Cuz, you already know shit is just as ugly out here. I lost two of my homeboys last week, and we in the middle of a war with them 18th Street fools. They trying to take over the whole town and make everybody follow them, but my crew ain't going." He frowned his face and shook his head. "My father is in the hospital. He had another heart attack last night and he's been unconscious ever since. I came back to get a change of clothes and lucky I did, or you would have been on the porch waiting for days. It ain't safe down here either, but my old man's house is off limits, just as is every other fool's parents. It's strictly gang against gang. All families are safe, for now," he added at the end.

Mami shook her head and felt sick to her stomach. She was so tired of all of the warring and killing. She wished things were different. She took a deep breath. "Look, my man going through some beef shit with a nigga that just killed his mother. I'm worried about him and I need for you to put him on with a little protection. He got heart, so it ain't sweet. He just need a place to regroup so he can handle his family business, then we shooting to Puerto Rico. I love him."

Berto smiled, looking her up and down. "What is it with you and black dudes? What, you don't like yo Spanish race?"

Mami waved him off. "It ain't nothing like that. I just care about him, and I wanna make sure he and his sister is straight. Well honestly, it's all about him, but she doesn't look like she's going to let him go anytime soon." She exhaled in defeat. "But it's good though. Right now, they're going through something, so I can understand what's taking place.

Berto frowned. "What happened to her face?"

Mami led him further into the kitchen, shushing him. "Will you be quiet? She's super insecure about her face. Her last boyfriend beat the shit out of her and did that. The wound is still fresh."

Berto nodded. "Oh, I didn't know." He lowered his head in deep thought. "Far as your man go, I'll fuck wit him if you want me to. I got enough guns to go around and if you guys are going to be staying here for a little while, then I'll get to know him. Ain't no harm in that, since you love him and all."

* * *

That night, Mami couldn't help tossing and turning. She had visions of her brother being killed. Somebody putting a gun into his mouth and pulling the trigger, blowing his head off, before they turned the gun on to Jahrome and pulled the trigger over and over again, killing him while she held him in her arms. She jolted awake and sat up in bed, screaming at the top of her lungs before she felt his heavy biceps surrounding her, pulling her into his heavy embrace.

"Baby. Baby, wake up. You okay, Mami. I got you. I'm right here. I got you, boo," Jahrome said, kissing her on the cheek. Mami turned to him and laid her head on his shoulder, then she looked over to his right side and saw Babygirl with her arm wrapped around his waist, very possessive.

She got out of the bed and pulled his arm. "Come here, baby. I need to talk to you. I need you real bad right now," she said, leading him into the hallway. Babygirl let him go reluctantly. She felt instantly alone and extremely jealous. She had visions of following them into the hallway so she could be near him. Anytime Mami wanted to be alone with her brother, it made her feel sick to her stomach. She hated sharing him. She threw the blanket over her head and cried her eyes out.

Jahrome looked her over closely. "Baby, what's the matter?" he asked, holding her beautiful makeup-free face in his hands. She was gorgeous. Her curly hair was all over the place. She smelled like sweat and traces of perfume. The expression across her face read worry. Mami pulled his hand until they got into the bathroom. Once there, she closed the door behind them and wrapped her arms around his neck, laying her head on his chest.

"Papi, I love you so much and I don't want nothing to happen to you. If anything ever happened to you, I'd kill myself right away. You mean way too much to me." She stood on her tippy toes and kissed his lips. Jahrome didn't know what she was talking about, but he didn't have plans on going anywhere anytime soon. He had too much to accomplish, he had to make sure she and Babygirl was well taken care of before he allowed anything to take place.

He felt like he had to be their protector, especially now that Mami's brother, and their mother was gone. Nothing else made sense to him. He trailed his hands down and cupped her big booty that jiggled under her nightgown, before squeezing it and biting into her hot neck. She moaned into his ear and spread her legs. "I love you so much, Jahrome, and I need you baby. I can't lose you and I keep on having all of these dreams that keep telling me I'm gone lose you, Papi." She leaned her head back and moaned with her mouth wide open.

Jahrome spread her thick ass cheeks and slid his two fingers into her pussy from the back, stroking them in and out of her hot opening. At every turn, her lips tried to keep his fingers inside. He bit into her neck and sucked on it loudly. "Ain't nothing gon' happen to me, baby. Not right now. I gotta make shit happen for you and my sister by any means. Once that happens, I don't give a fuck about what happens to me then." He rubbed his hand down in front of her and rubbed over her naked pussy lips. He could feel the hair was starting to grow back on them and for some reason, it turned him on like crazy. He smushed her lips together and squeezed them, until a thick glob of juices ran into his hand, before sliding off of his right wrist.

Mami moaned and tilted her head back further. "No baby, I'm saying I don't want anything to happen to you ever, or I'm gon' take my life because I would never be able to handle it. You got me gone in the head, Jahrome. All I need is you and I'll do anything for you with all I am." She felt him peel her lips apart and slide two fingers back into her, before pulling down the straps of her nightgown, exposing her succulent breasts. Both reddish-brown nipples popped up, looking like they belonged on a baby's bottle.

"Shut up and put one of them thick legs up on the rim of this tub. Let Papi eat this pussy, Mami, while you cry and release yourself into me. I know what you need, so do like I say." He bit into her neck and walked her backward until the back of her legs were against the tub, then she raised the right one and placed her foot on the rim, while he dropped down and licked up and down her left one. As soon as the right leg was in position, he pulled her gown up to her hips, exposing that brown pussy. Took his nose and put it between her sex lips, inhaling her scent and loving it, before inhaling her lips into his mouth while his tongue ran in and out of her body at full speed.

He peeled her lips apart and really attacked her kitty, sucking on her clitoris and running his tongue in circles around it, while he held onto her fat ass booty. "Huh. Unn-shit, Papi. Unn-shit, Papi. You're doing it again. You're doing it to me again, Papi. Oh shit, my Papiiii!" she moaned with her head tilted backward, grinding her pussy into his mouth as if she was trying to rub it off into it. She growled deep within her throat, feeling the sensations take over her body. Her eyes rolled into the back of her head and then the shakes came so bad, he had to hold her up while he ate her more and more until she screamed and fell against him. He picked her up and laid her on the floor, kissing all over her stomach and sucking the juices from her thighs and calves. She lay there shaking, with tears in her eyes. Loving him with all of her heart. "You're my Mami. I got you for life. Ain't nothing gone happen to me until I make sure you and Babygirl is beyond straight. Y'all deserve the best, and it's my job to make sure y'all get it," he said, pausing to suck all over her, sending chills up and down her spine.

She sat up feeling weak and drained, pulling him into her embrace with tears in her eyes. "I need you, Papi. I'm so weak. I'm tellin you right now nothing in this world matters to me because it's all about you, but I need to be first in your life, Jahrome. I need for you to love me first, Papi. Please. I understand she is your sister, but I'm your woman. You have to love me first." She saw that he was about to say something, but she put a finger to his lips, stopping him. She feared he was about to tell her nothing or no one came before Babygirl. She had heard him tell the woman that on numerous occasions, and she had always wanted to say something to him about that but decided against it because she didn't feel secure enough. And even though she was still having her insecurities, she was emotionally lost within him. She straddled him, reached backward and grabbed his thick pole, rubbing it up and down her pussy, until the head separated her lips and slid into her center. As soon as it did, her tears started to come down her cheek full bore. "I love you, Papi, please love me first."

In answer to that, Jahrome slammed her down onto his stick and humped into her, going as deep as he could into her hotness, while her titties wobbled on her chest. He grabbed her hips again and again, forcing her to take him deeply.

"Ride yo Papi, baby. Ride me and show me how much you love me. Prove this shit to me, baby. You know I need this body." He squeezed her titties together and sucked roughly on her nipples, pulling them with his lips until they were fully extended from her areolas. Mami closed her eyes and bounced up and down on him as if he were a horse. Plopping into his lap again and again, feeling his stick force its way up her channel, driving her crazy. She loved him so much. She needed him even more than he understood and every time he entered her body, it only made things worse.

"Unn-Papi! Unn-Papi! Please. Please, Papi. Please tell me you love me. Tell me you love me, Papi, and I'll do anything for you. I'll do it all for you, Papiiii!" She cried, sobbing and riding him faster. Her hips were a blur, her titties smacked against her upper stomach. The scent of her kitty wafted into the air.

Jahrome held onto her big booty and laid back, feeling her kitty grip him like a fist. It felt so good to him, so good he couldn't even think straight. In his mind, there was nothing like being ridden by a thick ass woman. One so strapped that it forced a man to bring out his A-game. "Ride this shit, baby. Ride Papi," he said, biting into his bottom lip.

"Unnnn-shit! Tell me you love me, Papi. Please. I'm begging you. I just need to hear it," Mami cried, riding him so fast they were slightly sliding across the floor. She felt him squeezing her ass and it excited her even more that he was even touching her in that moment. She needed more than anything to hear those three words.

Jahrome felt his nut building deep within him. He felt she needed him. Felt she had been through way too much in just a short amount of time and he owed her to be her healer. Even though he didn't really know if he loved her in the light that she needed him to, he felt strongly enough about her to give her what she needed. "I love you, Mami. You hear me? Papi love you, baby."

Mami started to shake so bad she couldn't breathe. "Unnn. Sheiiitttt, Papiiii!" she cried, coming all over him, before landing on his chest while his penis shot into her jerking again and again. Afterward, they laid on the floor while Jahrome kissed her all over, telling her how much he cared about her and how he had to make shit happen. She cried into his chest and listened to every word as if her life depended on it.

* * *

Babygirl sat with her back against the bathroom door with tears in her eyes. She felt left out and thought it was only a matter of time before they kicked her all the way to the curb. She had to make something happen, had to get her brother back in her favor. She couldn't stand to lose him to the likes of Mami. He was all she had and life without him seemed like a horror movie.

Ghost

Chapter 4

Lightning flashed across the dark Atlanta sky, sending an electric stripe that seemed to travel for a mile wide, before thunder rumbled overhead. Jock picked up the big brick and walked alongside Theresa's gangway, stopping in front of her patio door and lifting the brick over his head. Lightning flashed across the sky once again. He took the brick and threw it through the glass, shattering it, before he jumped through the frame with his .40 Glock in his hand, already cocked and ready to shoot.

Theresa jumped out of Derrick's embrace and thought about running up the stairs that led to the bedrooms. She was already convinced they were being burglarized and because she had come to this conclusion, she thought it was in her best interest to get to her locked gun. But before she could make it more than ten feet, Jock placed the beam from his gun on her forehead. "Theresa, if you move another fucking step, I'm finna smoke you and his punk ass," he said, upping his matching Glock and aiming it at Derrick. "Nigga, sit yo ass down."

Derrick raised his hands in the air and backed away from Jock. "Jock, what the fuck are you doing, man? Dymond ain't here." He continued to step backward until he was standing in front of Theresa. Theresa was Dymond's mother. He knew Jock was known for having a quick and lethal temper. He figured if the man was to start shooting, he would consume the bullets, sacrificing himself for his wife.

"Both of y'all get fuck on the ground. Now!" he hollered, taking a roll of duct tape from his pocket.

Theresa and Derrick slowly made their way to their knees, and then they were laying facedown. "Baby, we ain't never done nothin' to you. Ain't no reason for you to be treating good people like this," Theresa whimpered, fearing the worst. She closed her eyes and tried her best to remain calm.

In a matter of minutes, Jock had their hands tied behind their backs and sitting upright against the wall. He took a step back and looked them over. His gaze fell upon Theresa's wet face. He felt nothing for her, no sympathy whatsoever.

He lowered himself to one knee and looked into her brown eyes. "Theresa, you know I got a lot of love and respect for you. You been around me since I was a kid, and this really pains me to have you stuck in a fucked-up position like this, but shit is out of my control." He lowered his head and paused for dramatic effect.

Theresa began to shake like crazy. She didn't know what to expect. "Jock, please tell me what's going on? Are you high, or maybe drunk?"

Jock grunted and wiped his mouth with his hand. "Bitch, I'm both, but it ain't got shit to do with why I'm here." He cocked his gun and placed it to her forehead. "I need you to tell me where Dymond is right now. I know you know, and I ain't come to this muthafucka to play no games. Where is yo punk ass daughter?" he snapped.

Theresa shook her head. "I don't know. I haven't heard from Dymond in a few days. What could she have possibly done to have you coming at us like this?" Theresa asked, feeling sick on the stomach.

Jock pressed the barrel harder into her skin. "She stole a whole lot of money and product from me, and I ain't finna accept none of that shit, so you either finna help track her down, or I'm bodying you and him."

Derrick maintained his silence. He already knew he and Jock didn't get along. He didn't want to agitate him more than his presence already did. Sweat slid from his forehead into his right eye, burning it. He groaned out in pain.

Jock set his sights on the man. "Nigga, you got something you wanna add to this story?" he asked, feeling his heart began to pound in his chest.

Derrick squeezed his eyelids and laid on the side of his face. "Lil' nigga, you should already know I ain't got shit to say to you. I don't know where Dymond is and even if I did, it ain't my place to tell you a muthafuckin' thing. You need to get the fuck out of our home."

Jock's eyes were wide open. He couldn't believe the moxie of the older man. It both excited and infuriated him. He laughed under his breath and got into Derrick's face. "So, you tough, huh? You still think yousa young tough Bankhead nigga, huh?" Jock pressed his forehead against the man's temple. "Fuck nigga, ain't shit moving on Center Hill no more. Ma'fuckas over there don't even remember you," Jock teased, reminding the man of the fact that he knew what deck he used to claim. Back in the day, Derrick had been a well-known head bussah and dope boy. Nowadays, he was fifty years old, with a bad back and hypertension.

Derrick ignored Jock. Instead of responding, he turned his head to Theresa. "Baby, are you okay?"

Theresa nodded and exhaled. "Yeah, I'm okay, baby. I'm just afraid."

"Don't be afraid. We'll come from under this," Derrick assured her, even though he didn't believe that to be factual himself.

Jock grabbed a handful of the older man's hair and forced him to sit up, before he pulled a sharp pocketknife out of his inside coat pocket. He placed the blade against the side of Derrick's cheek. "Theresa, I need you to tell me where Dymond is. She done took a whole lot of my shit, and if I don't get it back within the next hour or so, I'm sorry but you and this fuck nigga finna have to pay the consequences. Now, where is she at?

Theresa shrugged her shoulders while laying on her side. "I don't know, Jock. I swear, I'm not lying to you." More tears fell from her eyes and down her face.

Jock poked a mini hole into Derrick's cheek. Derrick hollered out in intense pain. He banged the back of his head into the wall as blood dripped down his cheek. "How much you care about this nigga, Theresa, huh? Y'all been together what, ten years now? This nigga retired and settled into you. You mean to tell me you finna allow him to go out like this? Fuck type of wife are you?" he spat, sliding the knife across Derrick's face. Derrick hollered deep within his throat. As much as he hated to give Jock the satisfaction to see him in such pain, he couldn't help it.

"I don't know where she is Jock. I swear, if I knew I would tell you in a heartbeat," she swore, trying her best to sit up so she could see what Jock was doing. She was paranoid and thought him to be some kind of a maniac. She needed to keep her eyes on him and from her position on the floor, she was unable to see him clearly.

Jock allowed her to sit up. He slammed her back into the wall and resumed his place in front of Derrick. "Why don't you call that bitch, Theresa? Call that bitch and ask her where the fuck she is. I mean, unless you and Derrick are willing to sacrifice yourselves for her. Is that the case?" Jock raised the knife and brought the tip down into Derrick's cheek. After the knife slammed into its mark, Jock ripped it downward and hollered. "Arrgh, bitch, call her right now. I ain't playing' with y'all. Where the fuck is your phone?"

Derrick shook and fell forward. He was in so much pain he couldn't even think straight. There was a huge gash in his face. Both Jock and Theresa could make out his pink meat on the inside. His neck was covered in blood. Theresa pointed to the table. "My phone on the table. Bring it to me, Jock, and please don't hurt my husband any further," she begged.

Jock smacked Derrick as hard as he could, then stood up. "Fuck that tough ass nigga. He'll be alright. I never liked his bitch ass no way." He grabbed the phone off the table and knelt in front of Theresa. Threw her on her chest and cut her duct tape after a bit of a struggle. After her right hand was free, he picked up the phone and handed it to her.

Theresa opened her phone and went through the call log. She found Dymond's number and clicked on it. Placed the phone to her ear so she could hear when they connected. The phone went right to voicemail and what made matters even worse, her voicemail box was full. "Shit."

Jock mugged her. "I hope that's a good shit and not a bad one. It don't look like ya husband gone be able to hold on for too much longer." Jock eyed Derrick. Derrick sat with his head leaned forward, with blood pouring out of him at a rapid pace. Because of the blood thinners he'd taken, they caused his hemoglobin levels to be incredibly low. His open wounds were like a faucet.

"Her phone went right to voicemail, but I'm sending her a text right now. I'm telling her to answer her phone right away. Usually when I do this, she'll get back to me in a matter of minutes," Theresa assured him.

"You betta hope so, cause I'm giving you ten minutes and if she don't get back to you, I'm taking his ass out the game. Your time starts now." He walked over to Derrick and slapped his bloody face once again. "Wake yo punk ass up, nigga. This party seem like it's just getting started."

Derrick coughed up a loogie of blood and spit it on to the carpet. "Fuck you, Jock. Ain't nobody scared of yo punk ass."

Jock laughed and stood up. "Yeah, we'll see about that in minute. In seven minutes to be exact." He stepped over to Theresa. "Can you believe that bitch killed my daughter? Huh?"

Theresa was shocked and appalled. She just knew in her heart he couldn't have been referring to what she thought he was. "What are you talking about, Jock?"

"Yo punk ass daughter killed Aerial on some jealous shit, before she split with my money and work. That bitch gotta pay if it's the last thing I do." He grabbed her by the throat and added, "You better hope she call you in the next thirty minutes or I'm finna take my anger out on you and that fool."

Derrick coughed up more blood and wiped his mouth with the back of his hand. "You think doing some shit like this makes you a big man, huh, Jock?" He coughed some more and began wheezing for a moment. "I don't give a fuck what you do to us in here, in my book, you ain't nothin but a coward ass bitch." He hawked a loogie, blew it up, and into Jock's face. It landed just below Jock's right eye and slid off his cheek.

Jock was shocked. He wiped away the spit and turned his Glock around so that he was holding it by the nose. Theresa watched him beat Derrick into a bloody pulp. It took him all of five minutes to do so, and then he was standing up and stomping the man over and over again. "You. Nasty. Muthafucka. How. You. Gone. Spit. In. My. Fuckin. Face?" Over and over again he stomped him, until Derrick passed on.

Theresa screamed. "Nooooo, Derrick!" She crawled to his body and hugged up with him. "This ain't right, Jock. This ain't right and you know it." She rocked back and forth with Derrick's body, feeling powerless.

Jock checked his Rolex and saw they had been waiting thirty minutes for Dymond to get back to Theresa. He became even more furious. He wiped the gun on Derrick's clothes and aimed it at Theresa. "You think I give a fuck about what's right, and what's wrong? Your daughter killed my baby. It ain't finna be nothing but no mercy coming off of me until she answer for her sins. It is what it is. I always liked yo lil' thick ass. Theresa, damn what waste of flesh."

Theresa grew nervous. She looked up to him and scooted backward. She was covered in Derrick's blood. "No, please. Please, Jock. Please, don't do this. I am begging you!"

Jock stood over her and emptied his Glock. He watched as each slug entered her body. Glanced over to Derrick and saw he had already checked out of the game. Smoke drifted from his Glock. He shook his head and stepped over Theresa's body, determined to find Dymond.

Ghost

Chapter 5

"Aiight, baby, now let me just fuck wit' my cousin for a minute. This nigga got stupid clout down here in Miami, cuz he do that rap shit and been in the slums since day-one. I'm trying to get my foot in the game down here and the homie gone make sure I get put in the right way. But they don't be liking when women get in a man's business down here. That make it seem like the man is weak, and that'll make the homie looking at me sideways right away. And we can't have that, because we got a whole empire to build." He reached over and stroked her cheek with his big hand. "You know I'ma make shit happen for you, right? Like, you know I'ma give you that life you deserve and you ain't did all of this for nothing," Gunz asked her, looking her over closely. Dymond had been feeling sick, thinking about her daughter. Every time she closed her eyes, she saw the little girl begging her to not kill her. The image of her bluish face was burned into her mind for what seemed like forever. She looked over to Gunz and smiled weakly. She had so much faith in him. She had to because she was in way too deep now. Her life literally depended on his loyalty and how much he advanced in the game. Even though she was on the run, she still didn't want to live like a bum.

She was accustomed to a certain lifestyle and privilege. She took a deep breath and exhaled. "I know you got me. I believe in you, baby. I would have never done all I did if I didn't. You're my hero." He reached over and pulled her to him, kissing her on her thick lips. The sounds of their lips smacking together was loud in the car. Dymond moaned into his mouth, before placing her cheek against his. She could feel the scratchy hairs there. It was time for him to shave and she would make sure she found a way to tell him she liked her men with a little goatee. She wasn't really a major facial hair type of female. Gunz watched the big doors open up, before his cousin was standing before him with a big smile on his face.

"What it do, nigga? Long time no muthafuckin' see. Welcome to the palace," he said, putting both his arms in the air and moving out of the way so Gunz and Dymond could enter his mansion. As Dymond walked through the all-white doors, her eyes got bigger and bigger. The first thing she saw was two Brazilian women dressed like maids, standing behind Ross. Their hair was long and curly, and their uniforms were so tight that Dymond wondered how they were able to breathe in them. The skirts of the uniforms stopped just below their kittens, and their thighs were thick and golden. Their breasts were threatening to buss out of the tops and Dymond could tell the material was made so you could see their nipples as clear as day. She felt intimidated and prayed Gunz wasn't already choosing. She knew his cousin Ross was a major nigga in the hip hop world, but she never factored in what that meant.

"Ladies, this my lil' cousin right here and he's my guest and my blood, so treat him like you would me and be at his every beck and call. I mean that literally, and remember how he look right now, because a month from now my lil' nigga gone be eating out of the buffet of my city," Ross said, smiling and nodding his head at the same time.

Both thick ass women surrounded Gunz and ran their hands along his broad shoulders. They looked as if they were appraising his worth. Dymond got so jealous that she walked over to him and placed her back to his chest, before forcing him to wrap his arms around her. "I don't know what y'all used to, but this here is my man and if anybody gon' cater to him, it's gone be me. I'll kill over mines," she said, eyeing them evilly.

Ross rubbed him long beard and nodded his head up and down, liking what he saw. "I see Babygirl crazy about you, cuz. That's what's up. But you gon' have to tell her it's hard to cuff a man in this lifestyle." He put his hands in the air and waved them around, basically telling them to drink in his castle. Dymond saw the all-white marble floors and the two staircases, one on each side of the room that curved into a slight spiral. The mansion looked spotless. There were paintings all over the walls of famous black people. A big projector screen was pulled down in the next room that she could see from a distance. To her left and through the patio doors was a big swimming pool that looked like it could fit a hundred people. The water was the color of green mouthwash.

Ross gave them a small tour. She saw the kitchen was huge and slaving over the stove was another Spanish chick, with an apron and a white G-string that ran up her ass. She was braless with big perky titties. Her long hair fell down her back and rested on her big booty. On her feet were red-bottomed Louboutin's. She waved as they walked past, causing her left breast to fall out of the apron and expose itself. It looked wonderfully crafted. Dymond really couldn't believe her eyes when she saw an all-white baby tiger wander out of the back of the mansion, come up to Ross and lick his hand, before yawning and walking back off. "This is how you're supposed to live when you're a boss, cuz. This is how I want to see you eat, because you deserve the best, and fucking wit' me this how you gone be living. Now, step into my office," he said, putting his arm out and leading them down a row of stairs that turned the floor from marble into red carpet. As soon as they got down there, they saw a thick ass dark-skinned sista with a beautiful face and a banging body, vacuuming the carpet. She was so thick that every time she moved her ass would jiggle, along with her thighs. Her toes were painted black and green.

She was full-blooded Jamaican and represented her motherland to the fullest, just on her physical make-up alone. The more women Dymond saw, the more she started to ask herself what she had gotten herself into. She didn't see one female she could compete with in her mind, and that terrified her. After they sat down, they were brought umbrella drinks and Ross closed his office door. His office was huge, and a nice amount of gold and platinum plaques decorated the walls. On the shelf to the right of the plaques were three Grammy's. He rubbed his beard and adjusted his glasses on his face. "So, how may I be of service to you, beloved?" He nodded toward Dymond. "Before we get down, should we talk business in front of yo woman?"

He nodded. "She good. She do what I say."

Ross nodded. "That's the way it should be. I keep my women spoiled and well taken care of. The only thing I ask is that they stay in they lanes and stay out of my face until they're summoned. It's a man's job to make sure everything is taken care of. All I ask is at the end of the day they perform, because I'm worth it."

Gunz nodded. He loved his cousin's swag. His big homie was who he aspired to be like. In his mind, he had it all. Money, women, the lifestyle. He wanted his piece of the pie and he felt that Ross was the key to it all. He had the whole world at his feet. "Cuz, I wanna eat and I wanna eat so much that I burp. I got some merch with me and if I'm put in the right position, I can get rich and never have to look back. I just need your guidance and the key to yo city."

Ross smiled and looked him over for a second. "You gotta slow ya roll, daddy-o. Now, the last time I ran across you in the A, you was fucking wit that shiesty nigga, Jock. I ain't never liked that nigga and I know he got Meek chain snatched. I'm still looking into that situation." He curled his lip and made an angry face. Dymond swallowed at hearing Jock's name. It seemed like whenever a person spoke about him, it was always in the negative. He had so many enemies, it was amazing to her that he was still alive.

Gunz lowered his head. "I don't fuck with the homie no more. I'm ready to do my own thing. I'm ready to eat like you is, cuz."

Russ shook his head and pointed his finger into his mahogany desktop. "Now wait a minute. My eating come from hard work and because I paid my dues. I ain't just wake up like this. Everything that comes with this game comes from hard work and dedication." He stopped to sip from his umbrella drink. "I was a dope boy just like you. I was a young terrorist to them niggas on South Beach." He cheesed. "But now, I dine with' Lebron and argue with' the nigga Jay over the dumbest of shit. I'm eating because I played chess with the power players. I got this shit mastered because I calculate every single move before I make them. Every ma'fucka in this game got a proverbial chessboard sitting in front of them, lined up with pieces and they trying to mate every ma'fucka they feel that's sitting down in front of them. It's all about capitalizing off of the next man's mistakes so you can put yourself into a better position. You don't walk into this shit. You strategically force yourself into it." He sat back in his seat, opened a drawer and pulled out a fat ass stuffed Cuban cigar, before lighting the tip and inhaling a grayish cloud. He took two strong pulls and handed the blunt across his desk to Gunz. "This Loud here is courtesy of the big homie, Fidel."

Gunz took the blunt and inhaled deeply, thinking over the things Ross had said to him. He knew he was dropping jewels of the game and he tried to make sure he absorbed everything he was putting out. "What's your drug of choice, lil' cuz?"

Gunz pinched his nose. "I just toot a lil' powder every now and then. You know how that shit go." He felt the effects of the weed taking over him, making his mind cloudy. He jerked his head up to Ross and pointed at Dymond with his chin, asking him if he could pass her the blunt. Ross went back into his desk drawer and pulled out a strawberry Cuban cigar. It was all pink. He lit the tip and passed it to Dymond.

"I always make sure my ladies are welcome in my palace, but they are not to sip from my cup, nor are they allowed to smoke from my blunt. This is my garden. You women are my Eves, helpers and nothing more." He shook his head and smiled. "I wasn't asking you what drug you partied with, I was asking you which one you brought with you to get yourself a head start." He scratched into his beard before pulling on the hairs. "That's extremely important, because then I'll know where to set you up in my city."

"I got heroin and coke, but I'm strapped on that dog food. My shit pure and ain't stepped on, so I got a lot of work to do. No matter where you set me up, just remember I'm by myself, so I'm gone need you to set some hitters around me. Thorough ma'fuckas that's gone be all about they paper. I'm trying to rise out of these ashes."

Ross looked him over while pulling on his beard. He nodded. "I got the perfect spot and set-up for you. Some real niggaz that pledge their loyalties to me. I'ma do you this favor because I wanna see you eat. But just know, it's always gon' be one hand washing the other."

Gunz already knew that nothing in the game came for free. "By the way you saying that, I can tell that you already got something on your mind, so what's good?"

He smiled and hit a button on his desk, leaning his face into something that looked like a speaker. "Say, Bambi, I need you to come in here and snatch up my cousin's lady and have her fully pampered. I'm talking massage, hair, fingers, toes. I want the whole shebang. Show her how the boss get down, while I discuss some particulars with my blood." And that's just what happened, while Ross put Gunz up on game about how he needed a few niggaz knocked down to size that was coming into Miami that weekend.

* * *

Jahrome poured the last eighth of heroin into the aluminum foil, folded it and dropped it into a Ziploc bag with the other eleven thousand dollars' worth, before zipping it up. Mami wiped sweat away from her forehead with the back of her wrist. They had been up for the last four hours packaging dope and she was tired. She didn't understand how dudes could do that all day. She dropped the last pack into her Ziploc and slid it across the table.

"Huh Papi, that's eleven thousand, just like you asked me to do. I'm tired and I'm about to go take a nap. My cousin said he'd be back over this way in about two hours, so y'all can go to one of his traps and get down. Wake me up before you leave." She kissed him on the cheek and disappeared down the hallway, got to their guest bedroom and closed the door behind her.

Babygirl sat across from him with her head down in silence, bagging her dope. She paused for a second, adjusted her plastic gloves, then went back to work. She looked a little down, like something was bothering her. Jahrome looked down the hallway, then over to her. "Babygirl, what's the matter?" He sealed the Ziploc bag Mami had given him and sat it on the table.

She shrugged her shoulders. "I don't know. I just feel kinda blah today." She took a deep breath and exhaled slowly.

Jahrome took his gloves off and walked around the table, pulling her up to her feet and into his arms. He kissed her on the cheek and held her close. "You know I never liked when you were down. It always made me feel sick. Now I need to know what's going on, or shit finna be rough for me and since I gotta go out here and make it happen in a city I don't know shit about, I don't think that'll be fair. So talk to me, ma." She took her gloves off and scooted out of his embrace, looking down the hallway, trying to see if Mami had closed the door to the bedroom or not.

After confirming it was closed, she walked up to Jahrome and stood on her tippy toes, kissing him on the lips, wrapping her arms around the top of his neck, sucking passionately while moaning deep within her throat. He rubbed her back and lowered his hands to the small of her back, tempted to grab that big ass booty encased inside of white biker shorts. He broke the kiss with a loud popping of their lips. "So, that's what's been bothering you? You needed to kiss my lips?" He laughed and looked into her eyes.

She bit her bottom lip all sexy-like, before stepping forward, looking him in the eyes and sucking all over his lips, groaning deep within her throat. She placed her middle against his front so she could feel him better. Jahrome grabbed her booty and squeezed it with both hands. Her ass cheeks were fluffy. She still had that killer stripper body niggaz broke their banks for. Her booty felt hot, just like the kisses she was now planting all over his neck. He slid his hand down her biker shorts and felt her hairless kitten, separating the lips with his two fingers and sliding his middle one deep into her center.

She moaned into his ear and spread her thighs further. "That's what I need right there. That's what I want. I need you to fuck me, Jahrome, and stop playing with me. You always talking about you love me more than anybody else in this world, well why don't you love me like I need to be loved? Please," she moaned and licked his neck. He pushed her to the wall and pulled up her tank top, exposing her brown titties. Squeezing them together, before taking one erect nipple into his mouth and sucking hard on it.

He thought back to when they were little and after their parents went to sleep, how she used to always beg him to do that for her while she moaned for hours into the night. He nipped them with his teeth because he knew that drove her crazy. "Uhhh-shit, Jahrome. Fuck yeah. Fuck yeah, lil' bruh. I need you so bad." She started unbuckling his shorts, before sliding her hands into his boxers and pulling out his fat dick. She got it into her hand and squeezed it, before stroking it up and down. She dropped to her knees.

Jahrome looked down the hallway, praying the door didn't open. Babygirl had him all riled up. He knew she needed him, and he wanted to be there for her by all means. "You know what?" He pulled her up to her feet and picked her up into the air. She wrapped her legs around him, sucking all over his lips.

"I need you, lil' bruh. Please fuck this pussy. I know you love me, but I want you to love all of me. Please. I'm begging you," she whimpered.

He held her against the wall and tried to pull down her biker shorts. His mind was made up. "Babygirl, fuck that, get down and pull them shorts down enough so I can get in you. I want some of that pussy too. We all we got."

Babygirl damn near broke her neck pulling her shorts down. The material was wedged all the way up into her sex lips. When she pulled them down, she had to open her legs a little bit. As soon as they were down, she bent over the chair and opened her legs as wide as the cloth would allow her to. "Please, lil' bruh." Jahrome gazed at how fat her pussy was between her legs, before taking a deep breath, walking up to her and rubbing the soft material up and down her crease. She was so juicy, she leaked all over him before he could put it in. He placed the head on the opening and started to ease in real slow, looking down the hallway, praying Mami didn't open her room door. But then they heard the sounds of Berto's '64 Impala pulling up in front of the house.

Chapter 6

Jahrome took a step back and started to pull up his shorts. He hopped up, beef in hand and looked over to Babygirl, who was slamming her fist on the seat of the chair she was bent over as if it were a gavel. She looked pissed to him. Her light caramel face was a reddish hue. She stood up with her juices running down her inner thighs. She slowly pulled up her biker shorts and walked over to him with an angry look on her face, stood on her tippy toes, and kissed his soft lips. "We need to make this happen, Jahrome. I need you worse than I ever have in my entire life. That bitch shouldn't be getting none of you if I ain't. I'm supposed to belong to you first. Ugh." She shook her head and strolled down the hallway with her hand inside her biker shorts, stroking her kitty. Jahrome had her box on fire. She could still feel how it felt to have his fingers deep within her slot. She craved his forbidden touch. Jahrome heard her slam the guest bedroom door.

As Jahrome was situating his hard penis, Berto was slipping the key into the lock. Berto came into the living room with one of his homeboys, saw Jahrome sitting on the couch, and smiled. "What's good, bro? Say, I brought one of my homeboys with me for you to meet. His name is Paco. He's all about that paper just like us, and he's a hitta too. I grew up with him. The trap we finna fuck with that dog food out of is his uncle's place. He's a feen but it's good, because all we gotta do is hit him with a little bit of nothin, and we'll be able to maintain this trap as long as we wanna do our thing out of it. So, without further ado. Jahrome, this is Paco. Paco, this is Jahrome." Berto stepped back so both men could shake hands.

Jahrome shook his hand and nodded at him. "What it do, fool?"

Paco was heavyset with dark hair and brown eyes. He had a teardrop under his left eye and a small scar across his right cheek. "What's up, ése? I hear good things, homes. I hope they are all true. I don't fuck with many blacks." He released Jahrome's hand and took a step back.

Jahrome mugged him. "Fuck you say?"

"You heard me, homes. Why you looking all salty and shit?"

"Nigga, what?" Jahrome stepped into his face, clenching his teeth. He felt offended and irritated. He didn't know who the Mexican thought he was, but he was ready to show him it wasn't sweet.

"You heard what I said, homeboy." Paco's nostrils flared.

Berto stepped in between both men. "Say, y'all chill that shit." He mugged both men. "We're about to be getting money together. Ain't no such thing in us beefing. Paco, some things are better left inside of your head. And Jahrome, you ain't gotta run up in his face and shit. Now, let's sit back and figure out how we're going to get this money. Y'all cool with that?"

Both men continued to mug one another. "Are y'all cool with that?" Berto repeated. Both Jahrome and Paco nodded, each without taking their eyes off the other man. "Good, now y'all sit down, and let's develop a strategy to get this money. We gotta get it while the getting is good."

***

Jock took another huge bite from out of his gyro and sat back in the driver's seat of his blue Range Rover. He adjusted the vents in the car, so the cool air blew directly on him. It was ninety-five degrees outside but felt more like a hundred and fifteen with the humidity. He smacked loudly while he took in the scenery around Pamela's Red Hots. Most of the people going in and out of the restaurant were buying big ice cream cones, or milkshakes. The parking lot was packed with cars rolling in and out, and customers by the group load.

Jock sat back and couldn't help thinking about Aerial. He missed her little hugs, her laughter and her smile, and wished he had spent more time with her when she was still alive. Life was so short. He still couldn't believe how Dymond had betrayed him. How she had done what she'd done to their daughter. Every time he thought about it, it made him sick on the stomach. He was confident he would catch Dymond, and then he would make her pay for her betrayals and transgressions.

He grabbed the pop from the center console and drank some of it through his straw. His phone vibrated on his lap. Once again, it was Marvey. He knew what the man wanted without him even picking up the phone. He wanted his money and he wanted his work. When it came to Marvey, he was deadly. Jock knew he had to make a major move, and soon. While Reggie's killer, along with Dymond was still at the top of his list, he knew it was in his best interest to get his money up before he came under heavy attack by the Haitians.

Jock lowered his head and shook it. Once again, his daughter's image came across his mind's eye. His stomach felt as if it flipped over a few times. Suddenly, he became nauseous. He balled up the remainder of the gyro inside the wrapping it came in and threw it out of the window. Just as he was dropping it, a black-on-black Jaguar with mirror tinted windows pulled into the parking lot on the left side of him. At the same time that car was rolling into place, an identical Jaguar of the same make, model, and tints pulled up to his right side. The driver from the first car got out of his whip and tossed his long dreadlocks over his shoulder. Jock found it odd that the man would be wearing a long black leather trench coat, when outside appeared to feel like what he imagined hell must feel like. Jock thought the man was about to walk past his truck, and go directly into Pamela's Red Hots, when suddenly the man stopped and tossed back his trench coat. "Jock, Marvey sends his regards!" He came from under it with an Uzi that had a hundred-round clip attached to it. Jock dropped his head before the shooting started.

Boom-boom-boom! *Boom-boom-boom*! *Boom-boom-boom*! *Boom-boom-boom*! The bullets began to shred at his truck. The other men jumped out of the other two cars and proceeded to chop at Jock's truck as well. Their bullets sent the truck shaking from left to right. Glass exploded all over the dashboard and seats.

Jock stayed with his head lowered. He threw his truck in reverse and slammed on the gas. Through the onslaught of bullets he could hear people screaming. The bullets continued to chop at the body of his whip. He backed all the way up until he crashed into another car that was just coming into the parking lot. The sound of metal crunching was loud. Bullets continued to fly. Jock threw the truck in drive and stormed out of the parking lot. When he finally sat up, he looked in his rearview mirror, and saw the dread heads rushing into their cars. He stepped on the gas, nodding his head. He figured it out right then and there that Marvey had sent his hittas to take him out of the game. Every move for him from this point on would have to be crucial.

Chapter 7

"So, he gone let us stay in this whole wing? I mean, until when?" Dymond asked Gunz as he continued to help her counts the stacks of money they had taken from Jock's safes. They had been staying with Ross for three full days, and Dymond was low-key ready to go. She was tired of being around all of the good-looking females, with their flawless bodies and anything goes attitudes. She seriously worried about her and Gunz's relationship. She felt like it was in jeopardy the longer they stayed there. It didn't help that they had not been sexually intimate as of yet, and after being around all of those young flawless females, Dymond felt super insecure. She felt like every stretch mark on her body was a curse and would make him say "Ugh" out loud, which would crush her soul.

Gunz shrugged his shoulders. He really didn't feel like talking because it made him keep on losing count. "Yo, he ain't tripping and neither should we be. He wanna get me used to shit like this and I want you to get the same way. This is my stride. I want us to ball just as hard." He started to count again. "That nigga Jock sent me a threat too. I guess he know you ran off wit' me, so I gotta splash that nigga when I get time. You know how that shit go."

Dymond nodded. "To be honest with' you, I think we should have worked that into the grand scheme of things before we left. I been having all types of nightmares in regards to him. I know he ain't gon' take all of that shit laying down. I was wit' him long enough to know better than that." She lowered her head and shook it, thinking about how she had to kill their daughter and clean out all of his safes. She prayed he never found out where she and Gunz had fled to, because she knew that he had connections far and wide. There was never a moment where she felt safe as of yet.

She lined her piles of money up alongside the headboard. "Baby, I don't want to stay here though. I feel like we should get our own pad. These bitchez here gon' keep on tempting you, and that ain't gon' fare well for me." Gunz licked his thumb and continued to count the stack of ten thousand in his hand, before losing count again. It was impossible for him to count the bands and have a full conversation with Dymond. He'd lost count four times now and it was pissing him off. He lowered the bundle of hundreds to the bed and exhaled loudly, then looked over to her worried face. He knew what he had to do. She had invested too much into him and was the sole reason he was in the position he was in. He slid to the side of the bed and grabbed her to him, causing her to knock the pillow laying at her side onto the floor, kissing her on the neck. Dymond squealed before smiling and snuggling in next to him. She loved that he was so big he could just snatch her up anytime he wanted to without even asking. She was like most women in that sense.

He sucked on her neck. "Baby, tell me what you so worried about? Tell your man what's going on inside that mind up there and keep it uncut wit' me," he said, putting his hand under her shirt and rubbing her stomach. Dymond's eyes got as big as saucers. She didn't know why he had decided to do that. Her stomach was one of her insecurities, especially after looking over the other females in the mansion. She had a few stretch marks there from giving birth to Aerial and before she had come to Ross's mansion, she had really thought nothing of them. But after seeing all of the women that couldn't be older than twenty-one, with their flawless bodies, her small imperfection was getting the better of her. She moved his hand from under her shirt and stood up.

"I guess I'm just worried about you getting shit going down here, and then kicking me to the curb for one of these flawless beauties. I mean, I damn sure can't compete wit' them, and how long will it be before you peep that as well? Then what? Where does that leave us? Well, I know where that leaves you, but what about me?" She paced in front of him with her hands holding the small of her back, head lowered in deep thought.

Gunz stood up and snatched her up. Picking her up off her feet, making her wrap her legs around him while he held her there, looking into her eyes. "Look, I understand you got some mental things you have to deal with, because that nigga did a lot of fuck shit to you, but this ain't that. Shawty, I got you and I'll never forget what you did for us. I'm killing that nigga Jock on yo behalf, and I'm mastering the game out here on both of our behalf. I got you, I been feeling you since we were kids. These bitchez here all plastic, and they body parts leased. I'm feeling what I got real, right here in my arms. I wish you'd give me some of this body though. I been waiting for that. But, I know it's gone take some time, but when you're ready, I'm so-so ready." He smiled and kissed her lips.

Four hours later, Gunz found himself in the middle of his first piece of action on behalf of Ross. His orders had been, number one, no use of guns. Number two, to fuck over all three of the niggas. And number three, to make a statement so Ross could let the Miami underworld know it wasn't just about the rap, he was looking to conquer the dope game too and his word was bond. The niggas Gunz was hitting up owed Ross thirty stacks. He'd fronted them to make a few business investments that took off, but they never paid back. Instead, they took his money and theirs, and started a record company that had produced a few hitters and took to trashing the homie and his label. In his mind, that was double the disrespect.

* * *

Gunz grabbed Choppah by his neck and threw him against the wall so hard, it knocked the wind out of him. He slid down the wall and wound up on his side, struggling to breathe before Gunz raised his big foot and brought it down on to his chest, crushing his ribs. "Uhhhh, muthafucka," he groaned and started to shake on the floor.

Corky ran and jumped on his back, punching him in the head again and again. "Ahhh, leave us alone, you big bitch ass nigga!" he hollered, swinging with all of his might.

Gunz flipped him over the front of him and slammed him to the ground, pulling his knife out of the sheath of his waist, taking it, while holding him down and slicing across his face again and again. "Bitch. Nigga. When. You. Pay. Yo. Debts. When. You. Suppose. Too. This. Shit. Ain't. A. Game," he said, while he sliced the blade across Corky's face again and again. Not going deep enough to kill him, but enough to leave him scarred for life.

Those were his orders and he promised to follow them to the tee. Ross didn't want long investigated murders on his hands. He just wanted to make a statement to let hip hop and underworld know he was about that action. He'd already put on wax that he was gon' fuck them niggaz over, so it was heavily anticipated. He walked over to Racks, who was hiding in the corner wit' tears all over his face. He grabbed him by the throat, and he shit on himself.

"Man, I swear to God I'll pay Ross back. I ain't know this shit was that serious. I got money in the banks now. Please don't kill me."

Gunz swung and crashed his fist into his jaw so hard, he shattered it. Racks flew into the studio's glass with his hands into the air, knocked out cold. Gunz picked him up and threw him on the equipment before body slamming him to the floor. He looked over the trio as they laid on the floor groaning and moaning, taking his phone and recording it all. "Apologize to Ross and tell the world y'all some bitch ass niggaz! Now!" They didn't hesitate.

* * *

"Alright, that's the last bag right there. Now you sure your husband couldn't have helped you bring these in, Mrs. Jackson?" Jock asked, placing the last grocery bag on to her dining room table. She put her youngest grandson down and patted him on the butt as he ran into the house and disappeared in the back somewhere. She shook her head. "N'all, he's at work until late tonight. My son usually is the one that help me, but he ain't been answering his phone. I don't know what's going on," she said, closing the door and stepping into the house, before a car pulled into her driveway and blew the horn. She frowned and opened the door back, sticking her head out.

"Girl, I thought you said you wasn't coming back to pick him up until tomorrow?" Jock cursed under his breath. He was praying whoever was outside didn't come in. He had plans on slicing Gunz's mother up in a hundred different ways and posting that shit on Facebook. He knew he'd get the message then. Mrs. Jackson stepped to the side as her daughter Angel stepped into the house, along with her girlfriend. She gave her mother a hug and allowed for Queda to do the same. Mrs. Jackson hugged them both and turned to Jock. "Y'all already know who this is, am I right?"

Jock and Angel locked eyes and she lowered her head, then looked back up at him with anger written across her face.

Back in the day before she became a lesbian, Jock had been the one to take her virginity. He had told her everything she needed to hear so she'd lower all of her defenses. Then on her fifteenth birthday, he'd taken her virginity and never looked at her again. In her mind, he was a dog and she hated his guts. She had never told Gunz about it. She was too embarrassed because he had already warned her.

"This the famous Jock, right?" Queda asked, looking him up and down. She had heard about the story between her woman and Jock, and she didn't like him on the strength of that. She was also Ti's cousin, and word was out that Jock had something to do with his murder, so she ain't like him at all.

Jock smiled. "The one and only."

Angel rolled her eyes and crossed her arms in front of her. She was the spitting image of her mother, dark-skinned, with a pretty face and voluptuous body. "I see yo ego ain't changed none. What you doing in my mother's house, man? My brother ain't over here?" she spat and gave her mother a hug. Jock smiled and thought about saying something real slick that would hurt her feelings. But he decided against it because he knew there would be plenty time for that later.

"I came over here looking for my mans, then seeing he wasn't here, I saw Mrs. Jackson trying to carry all these grocery bags into the house while holding your son, and I thought it was only right I help her out." Mrs. Jackson hugged her daughter and then walked over to Jock and he put his around her, before kissing her on the cheek.

"And I'm glad he did too, or I would have been all day. I don't know what's gotten into Terrell, but he been real whiny since this morning."

Queda was super irritated. She didn't like how Angel's mother was allowing her girlfriend's ex to put his arm around her like he was doing. She felt jealous. "Well, it look like all the groceries in the house now so you can go, Jock, and I'll take it from here." She walked to the door and opened it up when Terrell ran from the back of the house and crashed into Jock, before landing on his four-year-old butt. Angel ran to his side and picked him up as the little boy started to cry with his mouth wide open. She put him into her arms and mugged the shit out of Jock.

"Damn, can't you see he was coming through here? Move yo big ass out the way." She held her son in her arms while he cried like a spoiled baby.

"Girl, watch yo mouth. Don't you see me standing right here?" Mrs. Jackson said, eyeing her in anger.

"I'm sorry, Momma, I just don't like him. It seem like every time he come around, something bad happens." She continued to console her son.

Jock laughed. "You have no idea."

Queda was over the whole scene. She felt like going to the car and smoking a blunt. "Look, I'm about to drive around the block and get some air. I'll be back in a lil' while." She was on her way out the door when Angel screamed. Jock was holding his pistol now, pointed directly at her.

"Bitch, get yo ass back in here before I pop you, and you see this silencer on the end of this foe nickel. That mean I can knock yo head off and won't nobody hear shit. Excuse my language, Mrs. Jackson."

Queda held her hands out in front of her and slowly closed the door. "Aiight, bruh, shit ain't gotta go down like that."

Jock walked over and snatched her by her shirt and flung her to the floor. She reminded him of a prettier version of Da Brat. "First things first. All y'all get on the floor on your stomachs and don't make me say it again. No disrespect, but that mean you too, Mrs. Jackson." He watched her drop down with her mouth wide open.

"Baby, what are you doing? You've always been kind to this family," she said, plopping down so fast that her summer dress wound up around her waist, before she pulled it back down.

"This is business. Yo son screwed me and my daughter over, so now I gotta pay it forward. You know how the game go. It is what it is." Angel tried to place Terrell on his stomach, but the little boy would not go. All he kept on doing was crying and stomping his feet, throwing a temper tantrum. Jock got irritated right away.

"Angel, pull that lil' punk down or I'm gone handle him in my own way. I ain't playing either."

"Don't you touch my son. You leave him alone. I'll take care of this," she screamed and tried to pull Terrell back down by his arms, but he snatched away from her and tried to run.

"No! I wanna go play on my tablet. I don't wanna lay down." He got ready to run to the back room when Jock snatched him up by the throat and held him in the air, choking him with one hand, while he held him against the wall. The little boy's feet dangled and kicked. He squeezed him harder and harder, imagining the fingerprints around his daughter's neck.

"Nooo! Please, Jock, don't do this!" Angel begged and got up on her knees, ready to dash at him.

Jock aimed and shot, the bullet ripping into her shoulder and knocking her backward onto her mother, with her blood running out of her. "Uhh! What the fuck?" she screamed, holding her shoulder.

Queda had seen enough. She refused to stay there and die like an idiot. She was waiting for the right time so she could try and escape. Jock had death in his eyes. She had seen that look many times before in a few other killers from her hood before they got down. Jock took the little boy and threw him against the wall with all of his might. *Whoom*! Picked him up and slammed him down on his neck, snapping it. The little boy landed with his neck on the ground, and his twisted body flipped all the way over.

Jock flipped his gun on safety and grabbed Queda by her long sew-in weave, before turning his gun upside down and crashing the handle into her face. Her head jerked backward, and he did it again but this time slamming it directly into her forehead, so hard it cracked it wide open. He knelt down and started to beat her senselessly, imagining Dymond choking his daughter to death.

It was because of her that he no longer cared about hurting women and children. Because of her and Gunz, this was taking place. He hated both of them and got pleasure out of what he was doing. He imagined his daughter, and his heart broke all over again. By the time he was done slamming the gun's handle into her face, Queda was long dead, her head turned to mush. A big pool of blood had formed in the carpet before he yanked Angel up by the hair. Angel was so scared her knees were knocking together. She couldn't even get the words out of her mouth to beg him for her life, because deep down she knew her pleas would fall on deaf ears.

Jock cocked back and punched her directly in the eye with all of his might, shattering her left socket, before dropping her to the floor. "Bitch, where yo brother at? That nigga got my money and my product."

Angel crawled backward on the floor with her eye swelling up and closing immediately. It had already turned blue. She was scared out of her mind, so much so she could barely breathe. She shook her head. "I don't know. I swear to God, I don't know where Gunz is. I haven't spoken to him in days and he ain't answering his phone."

Jock saw Mrs. Jackson starting to get up. Just as she made the move, he grabbed her by the head and slammed his knee into her face with all of his might, breaking her nose and knocking the older woman out cold. He pointed at Angel, before taking the knife out of his ankle holster. "Bitch, that's not what I wanted to hear."

Angel saw him pulling the knife out and saw how big the blade was. She jumped up, took two steps back and crashed through the patio glass door to try and escape. The glass door shattered around her loudly. She found herself on her knees on the deck, with shards of glass all in her face. She got up to run again.

Jock panicked. As soon as she jumped through the door, he was right on her, knocking away the glass she had left behind. He waited for her to stand up, then he cocked back and slammed the knife directly into her back and wrapped his arm around her neck, pulling her back into the house, where he held her against the wall and stabbed her in the stomach again and again. He made sure he was punching it into her gut. Cutting and stabbing as deep into her organs as the blade could reach, before he allowed her to drop to the floor with her eyes wide open. He knelt alongside of Mrs. Jackson, picked her up into his arms and sliced her from one ear to the next, before throwing her down roughly with a frown on his face.

Chapter 8

"Yo chill, that's how he always gets when he fucked up, bro. Trust me," Berto said to Jahrome as they watched his uncle lean all the way back on the couch and start to shake, with drool coming out of the corners of his mouth. Jahrome had been hustling with Berto for three days straight in the trap. He had not been to the other house where they were staying to check on the girls, because the money flow was so good. In just those three days, he had already made seven thousand dollars. Besides, he felt like he needed the time away from them so he could get his mind right, because he was going through so many things mentally that he needed to get a hold of. He couldn't help thinking about Mami a lot and he was sure he cared about her. She was someone special in his eyes and the more time they spent together, the more he knew he was falling for her like he never thought possible. Then, on the other hand, there was Babygirl. He felt like she would always be in constant need of him, and in a jealous state of mind when it came to him and other women. He didn't think she would ever accept Mami, because she truly thought she wanted him for herself, but Jahrome just figured she was emotionally and physically scarred and he was the only one she felt completely safe with.

He loved her with all of him and he knew he would do anything for her, but he felt like things were going in a direction he didn't know if he was ready to go in. "Yeah, well anyway, if that's how he get down that's cool. I'm about to ride back to the crib and see what's good with the girls. I been gone for a minute and both of them been on my ass about checking in, you already know hot that shit go." As he was saying this, there was a knock at the back door. He ran and looked out the back window and saw four dope fiends lined up, ready to purchase some of that boy.

Berto cocked his nine and took the two by four off the door. "What's good?" he asked, before looking back at Jahrome. "I'll holler at you in the morning, bro, and we'll break down the profit then. Text me when you make it to the crib and tell my cousin I love her."

Twenty minutes later, he was walking into the house and dropping his keys on the coffee table. Before he could even look up, he was bumrushed by Babygirl. She hugged him and walked him back into the door, wrapping her arms around the top of his neck, kissing his lips. He got nervous right away, looking over her shoulder trying to locate Mami, but it didn't stop him from returning her kisses.

Her tongue entered his mouth and he sucked on it, twirled his own tongue around hers, before sucking on her lips. She moaned into his mouth and pressed her crotch into his. "Why the fuck you ain't been back home?" she asked, hitting him in the chest and hugging him again, laying her head on the spot she'd just hit. Jahrome held her firm.

"Where is Mami at?" he asked, looking down the hall toward the room they were sharing together. Babygirl smiled.

"Aw, she didn't tell you? They called her into the club and promised her ten gees if she came and did her thing, because Quavo having his birthday bash there tonight. She won't be back until about four in the morning." She licked her lips, reached between them and squeezed his dick. "And I want me some of this. I ain't trying to hear nothing. I ain't got no panties on under this skirt, look." She took a step back and pulled up her black Gucci skirt, showing him her bald sex lips. "I shaved my pussy and everything because I want to feel all that you finna put down. I want you to do me good, just like you be doing her. Is that too much to ask?" She sucked on her bottom lip and looked into his eyes seductively. Jahrome saw the way her fingers played over her thick lips and couldn't help getting hard. He felt it was only so much a man could take. He stepped forward and moved her hand out of the way, rubbing her box himself. It was hot and seemed as if it were purring. Babygirl threw her head back and moaned, spreading her legs to give him further access. His fingers on her kitty lips felt so good to her that she was already starting to shake, but she knocked his hand away.

"N'all forget that, Jahrome. I want some of that dick." She started to unbuckle his Ferragamo belt, then his shorts. "I know who you is to me and I get all of that, but so what? I need you more than any woman in this world right now and I gotta have you. Please don't make me beg," she whimpered, already getting emotional.

Jahrome took a deep breath and in one motion, picked her up as she yelped in his ear, having been caught off guard. He carried her into the bedroom she slept in and tossed her on the bed, closing the door behind him, before taking his shirt off and dropping it on the floor. "You saying you want me to do you like I be doing her, right?"

Babygirl sat up on her elbows, watching him get undressed. Her fingers were between her legs already, opening her lips and pinching on her clitoris as she watched his abs come into view, along with his muscular chest. He looked like he worked out every single day. She knew he did a thousand push-ups every morning, and to her, it was doing the job. "Just like you do her, but with love, can you do that?" she asked, opening her legs wide.

Jahrome walked closer to the bed and dropped down to his knees, pulling her ass to the edge of it. "I remember all that shit you used to ask me to do when we were kids. Well, I'm grown now, and I know what I'm doing." Babygirl felt herself being pulled by her ankle, before his face disappeared between her thighs. She felt his long tongue lick up and then down her slit, before she felt him peeling her lips back and sucking on her clitoris hard, causing her to go crazy.

"Unnnn! Shit, lil' bruh! Oh shit, please do me right, baby. I need you so bad," she moaned as he slid two fingers into her kitty and started to run them in and out of her at full speed.

"You want me to fuck this pussy right? You begging me for this shit, right? Well I love you, Babygirl, but I'm not finna take it easy on you. Your brother is a savage. So, if you want me, you gone have to deal with this shit." He sucked harder on her clit and ran his fingers in and out of her at blazing speed, sucking harder and harder. He could feel her juices going down his throat and smell her scent going up his nose. It was all bringing the animal out of him, causing him to go insane.

She humped into his mouth and started to scream. It was too much. His lips on her clit, the fingers going in and out of her. The thought of who he was to her. Their play as kids. It was all going through her mind at one time and before she could control herself, she was shaking and smashing his face into her box with both hands. Jahrome kept on sucking, licking, and fingering as she shook. like crazy. He sucked up all of her juices, even taking the time to lick them off her thick thighs, before he stood up, and pulled her top down, exposing her pretty brown titties.

"I was obsessed with these. I used to love these titties so much that I used to dream about them. I remember every single time you asked me to suck them. Now they mine." He squeezed them together and started to suck one nipple after the next, while she reached between them and took ahold of his dick, leading his big head to her hole and guiding him in. Jahrome felt that heat and slammed it home, causing her to

70

scream, and wrap her legs around him for dear life. "Now, I'm about to beat this pussy in. It's tight too. Man, I'm about to kill this shit!" he uttered through clenched teeth, before pulling all the way back and slamming home.

Babygirl had tears in her eyes, as she felt him fucking her like crazy. He was a monster. He placed her thighs on his shoulders and went to town. "Unn! Unn! Lil' bruh! Lil' bruh! Please. Please. Please slow down. You fucking the shit out of me. You fucking the shit out of meeee! Unnn!" She felt the orgasm rip through her, and the tears came out harder and faster. Jahrome plunged deeper and deeper into her hotness and her walls sucked at him, trying to trap him inside. He leaned down and kissed all over her lips, sucking them into his mouth, before sucking on her neck.

"You wanted this shit, didn't you? You begged me for this dick. You just had to have lil' bruh hitting this pussy. Now, tell me you love it," he groaned, feeling like he was about to buss. Babygirl laid on her back, getting her kitty beat in and she felt like she was in heaven. She loved him so much. Every stroke, every plunge caused her to fall harder for him. She closed her eyes as another orgasm ripped through her, this time causing her to scream louder than she ever had before.

Jahrome felt her shaking, so he flipped her over onto her stomach and forced her to her knees, before getting behind her and fucking her from the back like a goon. He forced her face into the bed and dug that pussy out. "That's how Mami get that shit. This how I dick her down. This what you wanted, right? You wanted that uncut dick, am I right?" He plunged forward and took hold of her swinging titties, pulling on the nipples, while she came and came again all over his stick. Afterward they laid in the bed, with her kissing and rubbing his abs.

"I love you so much, Jahrome. I love you so fucking much. The things you do to me. I just don't know how to control myself, but I swear you're my everything. I don't want nobody but you." She was crying again, all over his stomach. She couldn't stop kissing it. He had her gone in the head. Jahrome was exhausted. They had been fucking for three hard hours straight. He wanted to make sure if they crossed that line, it was worth it and after the work they had put in, he felt like it was definitely worth it. He didn't have any regrets. He rubbed her back, before cupping her big booty, and squeezing it. Now he really understood how much she really had back there. "You good, Babygirl. You already know I love you, too. You're my everything, just like I'm yours."

She shook her head. "N'all, Jahrome. I don't think you really understand. I love the fuck out of you, to the point where if I can't be your woman, I'm ready to die. Fuck that. I want you to own me. I want you to tell me what to do and make me do it. My mine so gone right now, I can't even think straight. I just need you." She climbed up his body and kissed his lips, reached behind her and slid his piece back into her box, before sliding down on it with her eyes closed. "Ummm, shit." Jahrome pulled her down and kissed her lips, while she rode him slowly with tears running down her cheeks.

* * *

Ross sat back in his chair looking at the screen and nodded his head with a big smile on his face. "Now, that's what the fuck I like to see. Bitch niggas supposed to bow down just like that." He shook his head as he watched the action Gunz had handled for him.

"I told you this shit ain't a game, Ross. I'm willing to pay my dudes to make sure me and my woman stay straight. Any nigga you need taken care of, just point me in they direction. I'll handle that shit tonight." Ross looked him over in silence, rubbing his beard. A fat loud-stuffed Cuban blunt sat in the ashtray, fading away.

"You always had heart, my nigga, that's why I love you so much. But shit can't all be about business. Sometimes you gotta party, and I want you to fuck wit' me tonight and I'll show you how I get down. I wanna welcome you to my city as only I can, because I'm the mayor of this muthafucka and I got the game at my feet. So tonight, I want you beside me so I can introduce you to some of the power players that's gone be standing in your way. Just so you can get a feel. What you think about that?" he asked, picking up the blunt and taking a strong pull off of it, before blowing the smoke out of his nostrils.

Gunz nodded. "You the boss."

* * *

"Why you gotta go out and leave me here though? I already know that nigga finna have you fucking plenty hoez tonight. That shit ain't cool. I thought we were a team?"

Gunz continued to get his new Marc Jacobs 'fit in order. He looked like a straight boss. Clean and pristine. He slid the red-bottomed Jordan's on his feet and slid his jewelry around his neck, courtesy of the boss. "Everything I'm doing, I'm doing so we can buss into this game. I ain't looking to hurt you, baby. I told you I'm crazy about you. I meant that. Now, you gotta trust me more than you do." He continued getting dressed, took a nine-millimeter and placed it into the small of his back, before putting his matching Marc Jacobs button-up on over it. Dymond sat on the bed with her head down. She felt like there was nothing she could say or do. She was forced to let him be the man. She had to trust him and just hope and pray his loyalty was real. She bounced up and walked over to him, kissing his cheek.

"You know what, baby? I trust you and I believe in you, so go out there and handle your business. I'll be waiting for you when you get back and I want you to make love to me. I'll do whatever you want," she said, feeling more vulnerable than she ever had in her life. Gunz nodded and wrapped her into his arms. He didn't really know how to feel in that moment, because his mind was clouded by the prospects of getting his foot into the game. He didn't have time to dive into her emotions and felt he needed to stay focused on the task at hand.

Chapter 9

Ross popped the cork on the strawberry Ace of Spades, and the fizz bubbled over his fingers, before he sucked the juices off of them. "Here these niggaz come right now, lil' cuz." I want you to just lean back and be humble. They real arrogant because ain't nobody brought them that heat yet, but we gone change all of that. In order to take over a nigga's pit, you always gotta get rid of the snake that's lurking around in it. So, get a feel of these niggaz and then we gone fuck 'em over. You understand?"

Gunz nodded and watched the short white men walk over to the table, followed by their bodyguards. The first man, a short dude with long wavy hair that was slicked back into a ponytail, came over and extended his hand to Ross.

Santiago was a cocky Columbian who really didn't respect nothing black. He really didn't like Ross, but he gave him the time of day because he represented millions in his pocket. He made a mental note to scrub his hands after their meeting. He hated shaking hands, especially black ones.

"Hey big boy, I see you still feeding that face, huh?" he joked and straightened his Armani suit. Two big, beefy bodyguards stood behind him protectively. Sanchez stood five feet even, he looked like he was twelve years old, with a pretty boy persona. He shook hands with Ross and eyed Gunz closely. "Say, who do we have here?" asked the Columbian.

Ross curled his upper lip and tried to control his temper. "This is my new business associate and the man that's gone continue helping me, help you get rich," he said as the men sat down, where bottles of champagne sat before them on ice. They were at Giovanni's, a five-star gentlemen's club that catered strictly to millionaires and the upper crust of society.

In order to get into the club, you had to have a black card and a special recommendation from the owner. Mr. Benito Giovanni.

Sanchez snickered. "You think I need your help in order for me to get even more rich?" He laughed. "Yeah, like I'd leave my fate in your hands.

Santiago took a long swallow from his champagne. "You give these niggers a foot and they think you owe them a mile." He laughed to himself and slammed the bottle of champagne down so hard, the liquid flew into the air and landed on Gunz's cheek.

He was so irritated he didn't even wipe it off, and Santiago didn't apologize either. "The only thing I need you for is to be the cover of my book when I pump my drugs into your people. They need a nigger to look to. Somebody they aspire to be like, whose words are golden. You're supposed to be the boss," he said, laughing and doing little air quotes with his fingers.

Santiago laughed at Sanchez's joke. "Could you imagine this guy being the boss of something? Fucking ridiculous. How dumb they must be. Like the world would ever really allow that. Obama wasn't even the boss when he was in office."

Ross slammed his hand on the table. "Fuck all that silly talk, homeboys." He mugged one and then the other as Sanchez smiled and took a swallow from his champagne. "Now, the reason why I called this meeting is because I wanted y'all to meet my new partner. I need for him to be fully acquainted with the bosses, because I'm about to be out of the country for a few months, and I'm gone put him as head of a few of my operations. So, I'd appreciate if you fools would show some respect, just like I'm giving you."

Sanchez shrugged his shoulders. "Nah, no thank you. What else you got, because you know how this shit goes, and this person here better figure it out right away," he said, wearing a disgusted expression. "I am who I am, and that won't change for some monkey. It's a reason why your kind is the lowest on the totem pole," he spat, and took a swallow from the champagne.

Gunz felt his heart beating fast. He was ready to knock one of their heads off. He looked behind the men and up to their big and beefy, heavily armed bodyguards, sizing them up. They were stone-faced and looked evil. Santiago smiled and laughed deep within his throat. "What are we talking?"

Ross could barely breathe. He had a forty-five in the small of his back and was trying to remain calm. He had visions of shooting both men at point-blank range, head shots and he'd suffer the consequences later. But then he remembered he had to stick to the plan. It was all about the best move on the chessboard, one move at a time. He cleared his throat. "That China boy, two districts, east and west. My man is a fool with that heroin, and he know how to increase profits. I checked the history and he valid."

Sanchez nodded and mugged the shit out of Gunz. "What he saying true? You know your way around some horse? Huh?"

Gunz barely wanted to acknowledge him. He felt like the man should have been dead on a slab somewhere, with a tag on his toe. He looked to Ross and he nodded. "Everything the homie say is true."

Santiago turned his head to the side. "Oh, we got a man of little words. I like that." He smiled at Ross. "You got yourself a little lap down here, huh? What, you're his boss?" He shook his head and took a sip of the champagne. "That still tickles me."

Ross stood up. "Just know that for the next few months, me and my mans finna go real hard on moving this product, so all of the Columbians you been slowly moving into our slums, it's time you move them out. We'll handle our own people, that's that. This meeting is adjourned."

Sanchez looked up to him with hatred. He hated when people stood up while he was still sitting down. "Sit your ass down, boy, I don't like when gorillas tower over me."

Now Gunz was heated. He wanted to see what Ross did. He didn't think his big homie would allow the man to talk to him like that.

He knew from experience that Ross had a bad temper, just like he had. When they were kids, they often fought groups of niggas together. He refused to believe he was about accept what the Columbian was putting down.

Ross curled his upper lip and pulled on his beard, looking down at Sanchez for a long time with a sly grin written across his face. "Gunz, let's shake this joint lil' homie, before we leave a bad taste in their mouths."

Gunz sat there for a while longer, before rising and looking down on Sanchez, mugging him, hoping and praying he made a comment like that toward him. He didn't give a fuck what Ross was talking about. He was gone put a bullet right in his forehead and start melting away the other Columbian's face as well. He hated them, just like they hated him. After they made it back out to the limo, he couldn't help but to feel angry. His blood ran hot. His temper was getting the better of him. "Ross, what the fuck was that, man! How we gone let them talk to us like that? You should have let me murder they bitch ass. We don't bow down to no man, especially not them puny ma'fuckas." He slammed the limo's door and plopped back into the seat.

Ross lowered the partition in the stretch Navigator. "Me and my man's going to First Class Divas, on the strip. Take the port route." He raised the partition and smiled, grabbing a bottle of raspberry Moscato. "Everything I needed you to see, you saw. Every feeling I needed for you to feel, my nigga, you feeling it right now, but your emotions are all wrong and your thinking is twisted. You can't outthink the man on the other side of the board if your brain is clouded from anger due to his last move. It's all about capitalization. We see the Columbians are big-headed. They're bullies and when a ma'fucka's head is too big, they can't see their feet and if you can't see your feet, you can't watch where you're walking. Now peep our next move."

* * *

By the time Mami got home, Jahrome was exhausted and wore out. He was freshly showered and snoring like a bear when she slid under the covers and rubbed his chest, before biting it to awake him. Babygirl was beside him, laid out in her Victoria's Secret pink boy short set. She snored only lighter than he did, but her sleep was just as deep. Mami felt some type of way. She felt jealous because while she had been gone, Babygirl had been able to sleep in her place. She swallowed and felt her stomach turn. She pushed Jahrome again until he slowly opened his hazel eyes. "Wake up, Papi. I'm home, and I missed you." She kissed him on the lips and rubbed her face against his.

Jahrome's eyes slowly adjusted and when Mami's face came into full view, the first thing he thought about was Babygirl and being naked right next to him. He looked to his left and was about to pull the covers over her, when he noted she laid there sleeping and clothed. He took a deep breath and exhaled. "Hey, Mami." He kissed her lips and sucked all over them with his eyes closed. She smelled amazing to him as usual. She held up a fat knot of money.

"Huh, Papi, this is yours. It's damn near eleven thousand dollars and I just made this tonight. I want you to have it, because I see what you're trying to do for us, and I respect it. Any way I can contribute. I feel like it's my job to help, so that's why I got up and made shit happen without telling you, because it's my job to do exactly that." She kissed him on the lips and nuzzled her face into the crux of his neck.

Jahrome took the money and counted into over her back while she laid down. He couldn't believe she had brought back so much paper in one night. He had been hustling a few days and only nearly came to that amount. Impressed, he sat up and looked over at Babygirl, then back at her. "Mami, I love that grind you got inside of you. You just like me and that makes you official. You're my baby, you hear me?" He tongued her down, while she moaned into his mouth, her long curly hair falling over his fingers as he held her.

"Papi, I been through a lot of bullshit tonight. All of that pawing and groping, and men ogling my body, just makes me feel so sick now. I felt like I was cheating on you or something, even though I will never get down like that. I just want you to hold me for the rest of the night. I need for you to let me know how much you love me and care about me, because I'm feeling so weak right now. Can you do that for me, baby?" she asked, scooting onto the bed and under his embrace.

Jahrome kissed her on the forehead. "Of course, I can. Turn around so I can hold you like I'm supposed to." She got out of the bed and pulled her tank top over her head, then slid her tight capris down, and got back into the bed in just her G-string. Laying her back to his chest, she lifted his arm and made him put it around her.

"Papi, did you really miss me?" He kissed her on the back of the neck.

"Of course I did, baby. Every time you ain't in my presence, I miss you. You're my Puerto Rican queen." She wiggled her hips until her ass was lined up with his dick. She could feel it laying across the lower portion of her booty cheeks. It was hot and throbbing, just like always.

"The reason I ask you that is because before I left, you was gone almost three days and you never came home. I would never be able to stay away from you like that, unless you make me, just like you did this time. For the record, I don't like when you tell me to do shit like that. You're my man and I wanna be under you as much as possible. That's my right." She closed her eyes and couldn't get the nagging feeling from Babygirl being in the bed, out of her head. "Jahrome?" He placed his face into her hair, inhaling her precious scent.

He always loved how she smelled. She had that distinct essence that drove him crazy. "Yeah, Mami?" She rose and looked over his shoulder to make sure Babygirl still had her eyes closed. After confirming she did, she laid back against his chest. "Why is she sleeping in here? She taking my place?" she asked with a lump forming in her throat. She didn't know if she was ready for his honesty. She braced herself, just in case he said the wrong thing that would shatter her.

Jahrome shook his head. He didn't want to get into an argument with her in the middle of the night, especially after they had been apart for nearly three days straight. "Baby, can't nobody take your place. Your slot can't be filled. Now, I love you and I don't want to do this right now."

Mami swallowed. "The most though, Jahrome?" He frowned his face and opened his eyes to look at the back of her head. The moonlight shined through the window in the bedroom, illuminating it.

"The most what, Mami?"

She sat up a little bit and turned around to look at him in the face. She could now feel his penis laid up against her front, her small panties doing very little to protect her from his heat, even though he was wearing boxers. "I mean, do you still love me the most like you said? Like, am I your one and only love?" She felt herself starting to panic. She needed him so bad. Emotionally, she was out of whack. She saw the way the men at the strip club pawed all over the other girls, herself included, and it made her think about how trifling men really were. She was sure more than eighty percent of them were going home to their women after doing all of that, and it made her feel insecure within her own relationship. She needed to know he loved her and that he loved her the most. Jahrome didn't want to get into all of that. He loved Mami, but the truth was he didn't love anybody more than Babygirl.

She was his everything and they had been through way too much together, from the time they were kids, and even as adults. They had just lost their mother and he knew deep down, nobody needed him as much as Babygirl did. "Mami, you know I—"

Before he could even finish his sentence, Babygirl sat up. "Why don't you want him to love me? Huh? Why the fuck would you be his one and only love, when I been a part of him his whole life? Huh?"

Mami got out of the bed and turned on the lamp, her naked breasts bouncing on her chest. "Yeah, let's just do this shit, Babygirl. Let's just get it all out of the way, because I'm tired of walking on eggshells around yo ass."

Babygirl jumped out of the bed with anger written across her face. The Victoria's Secret number was so small she could barely move as she walked over to Mami and stood less than an arm's length away from her.

Ghost

Chapter 10

"You think you gon' take my place? You think after all me and him been through, since you just waltzed into the picture with yo long curly hair, and yo lil' thick body and perfect face, that Jahrome just gon' forget I even exist, huh? Girl, bye." She rolled her eyes and crossed her arms across her chest.

Mami took a deep breath and exhaled loudly. "I don't understand this shit, I don't understand why I can't be his woman and you just be his sister? Why am I competing with his fucking sister? Like, does that make any sense to you whatsoever?" she asked, tapping a finger on her temple.

Jahrome came over and wrapped her in his arms. "Look, it's too late for this shit. Y'all need to chill because shit getting blown outta proportion. Now, you are my woman and she is my sister, and ain't nothin gon' change that. Y'all just bugging right now." He started to lead Mami to the bed. Babygirl shook her head. She was furious. She wondered why he chose to console Mami and not her. Didn't he understand that she was just as mad? That she felt just like Mami felt, but maybe a little worse, because she had been a part of him his entire life? She wondered why he didn't get that.

"N'all, fuck this. I'm ready to fight over my brother. I can't compete with this pretty ass bitch. Maybe before this shit happened to my face, but not now. I can't lose you, Jahrome. So, far as I'm concerned, me and her can fight it out and the losing woman should walk the fuck away. But I'm telling you now, Mami, I'm willing to die for him. He's all I got, and I love him with all of my heart. So, let's get it on." She took a step back from the bed and put up her guards, causing the tube top to raise and expose the bottoms of her breasts.

Mami scrunched her face and jerked away from Jahrome. "What, because I'm pretty, I'm supposed to be scared of you?

All my life, bitchez been trying me because of how I look and I ain't lost many fights. I ain't won 'em all, but I damn sure won more than I lost. So, let's go, Babygirl. I just want you to know I do care about you, but I care about yo brother more. He's my man and not yours. I'm his woman. You're his sister, and he only loves you like a sis-ster," she said, drawing out the word purposely. By this time, Babygirl was in tears and her heart was aching. Every time she'd called herself his woman, it stung.

Every time she looked her up and down and noted how pretty Mami was, it bruised her. Every time she peeped how Jahrome was still standing behind Mami and not her, it made her want to die. Suddenly, she felt like the ugliest woman in the world and the scar on her face felt like it was vibrating to announce her ugliness. She hollered and smacked Mami so hard, the woman flew backward into Jahrome's arms and then both of them fell on the bed. "You stupid bitch! You trying to make him love you more than me. Well, if I ain't got him, then fuck this life. Ahhhh!" She ran over and grabbed Mami by the hair, yanking her off of Jahrome. Mami felt her pulling her by her curls, and it hurt so bad all she could do was wince in pain, before falling to the floor. Babygirl straddled her. "I thought we was cool, but all you care about is taking him away from him, you pretty bitch. You can have any man in the world. Leave mine alone!" she screamed and wrapped her hands around her neck, squeezing.

Jahrome hopped up and pulled Babygirl off of her. "Sis, chill, you going crazy right now. Everybody good. Y'all blowing this shit out of proportion for nothing." This was the last thing he wanted to happen. He wished he had never gone there with Babygirl. He didn't want her fighting with Mami, because deep down, he truly cared about her and saw himself being with her for a long time. He picked Babygirl up into the air and then placed her on the bed. Mami stood up and ran her fingers through her hair, looking at both of them and shaking her head. The Puerto Rican in her told her to go and grab a knife to slice Babygirl's ass up. But, underneath it all, she still didn't want to lose Jahrome. She had fallen way too deeply in love with him already.

"Jahrome, I need for you to let me know what's going on. Seriously." She watched him struggle with Babygirl on the bed. The woman had tears in her eyes. She looked as if she wanted to get out of that bed and really get at Mami. Mami had no idea it was that serious. She couldn't think of anything she had done to the woman to make her feel so angry toward her.

Babygirl twisted this way and that. She was tired of Mami being around. She wanted Jahrome all to herself. She couldn't compete with Mami. She was too bad. She saw the way Jahrome looked at her and it killed her soul. "Let me get that bitch, Jahrome. I'm tired of this shit. It hurts too bad."

Mami stood there with tears running down her cheeks. All she wanted was to be able to be a good woman to Jahrome. All she wanted was to be able to love him and he love her unconditionally. She understood Babygirl was going through a lot, but she didn't feel like it was fair for her to take things out on her. She slowly started to get angry. "You know what, Jahrome, let her ass go. Fuck that. I'm tired of being the nice one." She pulled her hair back and wrapped it around itself to create a ponytail, her breasts bouncing while she completed her task. Then something in her snapped. She reached and grabbed Babygirl's leg and yanked her out of the bed. She fell on the floor, on her ass. Jahrome jumped back and shook his head. "You know what, I ain't finna go through this shit. Y'all gon' fight, get that shit over wit so we can be adults from here on out."

Babygirl felt Mami grab a handful of her hair, and then she slapped her across the face with an open hand, before throwing her head against the bed. It bounced off the side and caused her neck to pop. Mami took a step back and frowned. "Get yo ass up, mamita. Sabes que, it ain't sweet. You wanna fight for him, well let's do it, because I love him just as much as you do."

Babygirl jumped up, lowered her head and ran full speed at Mami, swinging her arms wildly like a windmill, fucking her up. She hit her so many times that Mami fell on her ass and hopped right back up. "Come on, bitch. You ain't said shit," Babygirl hollered, with her chest heaving up and down.

Mami bit into her bottom lip. "Yeah, yeah, okay bitch, let's go then! Ahhh!" She closed her eyes and started swinging crazy like in Babygirl's direction. She hit her in the forehead, in the ear and finally in the chin, knocking her out cold, but she didn't know it because her eyes were closed. She kept on swinging until she ran out of breath, only then did she stop and open her eyes. When she saw Babygirl laid out on her side, her eyes opened wide before she dropped down to her knees. "Holy shit. Babygirl, are you okay, mamita?" Babygirl was out like a light. Her head rocked from side to side and there was a little drool leaking out of the corner of her mouth.

Jahrome knelt down beside her. "Damn, Mami. Y'all crazy, fighting for no damn reason. You my woman and she my sister, ain't shit finna change that. Now we gotta deal with' this shit. You already know she finna be on some vengeful shit." He frowned at her and it hurt her deeply.

"I just love you that's all, Jahrome. I love you with all of my heart and I'll do anything to anybody over you. I mean that shit."

They heard a car slamming on its brakes in front of their house, before there were footsteps on the porch, and then the sounds of a key jiggling in the lock. Jahrome ran to the bed, and grabbed his forty-five from under the pillow, cocking it back. "Make sure she straight. I'm finna go see what's good up here."

Mami nodded and he stepped into the hallway, closing the door behind him. He lowered himself as close to the floor as possible, with the gun raised pointed toward the front of the house. When the lights flashed on and he saw Berto's worried face, his eyes bucked before he put the pistol down. "What the fuck going on, bruh?"

Berto pulled Jahrome by the arm and brought him into the living room where he fell on his knees in front of a little girl's body. "This my little cousin, man. They shot her trying to hit me. They killed her, Jahrome. She was only six."

He picked her up into his arms. His face and entire shirt were covered in blood. Jahrome looked down on the little girl. She had a hole right in the center of her forehead and another one right in her chest. Jahrome shook his head, he couldn't understand how anybody could do that to a little kid. Jahrome always felt like when it came to that beef shit, he would leave it between men, unless a female picked up them hammers and wanted to try her luck. Then, all bets were off. He knelt on the floor beside Berto and picked up the little girl's hand, feeling a deep compassion for her. Mami waltzed into the living room, saw Berto and then looked down, noting all of the blood. "Oh my God! Who is that, Berto? Please tell me it isn't who I think it is?" she screamed and ran all the way to them and dropped down, before breaking out into a loud sob. "Manuela! Nooo! How did this happen? She's only six years old."

Berto rocked back and forth with her in his arms. He cried and tried to get ahold of himself. "It was Hector and Suave. I saw both of them fools clear as day. They were so crazy they didn't even have any masks on. We were at Subway. I was getting out of the car when they rolled up. When they rolled up, and…" He broke all the way down.

Mami placed her arms around his shoulders and cried into his neck. Manuela was her favorite little cousin, their cousin Melissa's only child. She was smart, quiet and very well-mannered. Mami didn't know if Melissa knew about the murder or not, but she knew whenever she found out about it, she was going to take it hard.

Jahrome looked up and down the hall and saw Babygirl standing there looking in on them. She looked angry and he noticed she had a big butcher's knife in her hand. He shot up from the floor and met her in the hallway. As soon as he got close to her, she held it up in a threatening manner. He paused in his tracks. "You love that bitch more than me, don't you?" she asked, with her eyes low. "They're going to be your new family and I'm going to be kicked to the curb, ain't I? I'll be all alone without you, won't I?" Now she was crying and taking deep breaths.

Jahrome put his gun on his waist and held his hand out. "Babygirl, give me the knife and stop talking like that. I already told you I will never leave your side. Now stop this. It's a dead little girl in there," he said, getting a little frustrated because he felt they shouldn't have been going through this at the time.

She shook her head. "I don't care. There's a dead little girl right here too, Jahrome and you don't even see it. All you see is these Puerto Ricans. You don't even see me anymore. You let this bitch put her hands on me and when I wake up, y'all in there all lovey-dovey and shit. I can't take this, man. I'm not strong enough."

He stepped forward and knocked the knife out of her hand, cutting his fingers in the process, snatched her up and carried her into the room he and Mami shared together. As soon as they were in it, he closed the door behind them and pressed her up against the wall with a thud. "Now listen to me, Babygirl, me and you are forever. I love you with all of my heart and that will never change. All I see is you and nobody will ever take yo place. Get that shit through yo head, or you're going to be the cause of our downfall. Now, they lil' cousin just got bodied and I need to be there to support Mami. It don't mean I love her more than you, but she is my woman. I'ma need for you to get grown real fast and honor that shit. I got you, but you still my sister." He frowned in anger. "You hear me?"

Babygirl couldn't hear or understand anything he was saying after he had slammed her into the wall. The only thing she kept saying over and over to herself was, *I need to kill Mami and get her away from Jahrome. It's the only way I'll be able to have him all to myself.* Mami ran into the room and bussed through the door.

"Jahrome, Hector them just pulled up out front with three cars. I think they finna kill my cousin. You gotta do something," she hollered before dropping to his feet.

As soon as she dropped down, they heard the gunshots, six in a row and then the sounds of the windows blowing out in front of the house. Jahrome pulled his gun from his waist and ran into the hallway. Berto must have laid the little girl's body right by the door, because he almost tripped over her, but jumped at the last minute, slightly freaked out.

He looked down the hall and saw Berto kneeling down with tears coming from his eyes. They made eye contact. Jahrome waved for him to follow him. Bullets continued to fly from Hector and his crew that were parked in front of the house. Berto low crawled down the hallway until he was right in front of Jahrome. Jahrome helped him up and they went running into the kitchen, and out the back door of the house.

"Bruh, come on, we finna sweat these niggas from the gangway," Jahrome hollered, taking off along the side of the house. Berto tried his best to stay in tow but he felt sick from Manuela's murder. He didn't know how he was going to explain it to his cousin Melissa. When they got to toward the front of the house, Hector was just running around to get back into the driver's seat of the van when Jahrome, and Berto started shooting at him, and the getaway van. Both men finger-fucked their triggers with fury. But it was too late. Hector made it inside the van and smashed away from the curb, sending smoke drifting from the tires. Jahrome ran into the middle of the street still bussing at them, his bullets appearing to miss altogether.

Berto lowered his gun. "We gotta get them niggas, Jahrome. They killed my lil' cousin. We gotta holler at them like, ASAP!" Berto snapped.

Jahrome agreed. "I'm wit' you, bruh. Come on, let's go make sure the girls are straight."

Chapter 11

Jock dipped his nail into the tin foil, scooped the heroin, and tooted it hard up his nostril. He repeated the same process, before leaning back in his driver's seat, adjusting the gauge 2. on his lap. He knew the regular routine of the Haitians and who they fucked with in Atlanta. Jock had been trailing behind Beanie for the last few hours, waiting on him to make the last stop on his route. He watched him walk out the back of the housing complex, looking both ways, before chirping the alarm on his BMW, opening the door and climbing inside. Jock knew he always sat there for a moment and confirmed he had made a drop for Marvey before he drove off.

Jock smiled and licked his dry lips. He felt the heroin cruising through his veins. It had him feeling pain free and breezy. He looked out and noticed there were all kinds of people around, coming to and from the housing complex, going on with their days as if they didn't have a care in the world. He pulled the mask down on his face, opened his truck's door and dropped down. Beanie was parked three spaces over in the back of the complex, in front of a big metal garbage can. He crouched down and ran as fast as he could, and then popped up on Beanie's driver's side window with the gauge pointed directly at him.

Beanie looked out his window and by the time he saw Jock, it was too late. There was a loud boom and then fire spit from the barrel of Jock's gun. Beanie felt the round slam into his face, knocking him back on the seat. Jock cocked the gauge and shot again. *Boooom!* Splitting Beanie's face in two, his blood splattered all over the interior of the car. "Bitch ass nigga!" Jock reached into the car and grabbed his cell phone, before wiping it on the man's clothes. "Hello! Bitch nigga, hello!"

"Who da fuck iz dis? Ya fuck wit' me? Ya wanna fuck wit' me, rite!" Marvey said, sounding heated.

Jock laughed. "Bitch nigga, this is who you think it is. I ain't paying you shit. Kill me before I kill you. I see anything Haitian around my hood, I'm chopping it down." He ended the call, reached in and grabbed a wad of money from Beanie, before hopping in his truck and skirting away from the scene. He didn't even give a fuck that there were at least fifteen witnesses that had seen it all.

* * *

Gunz stepped through the yellow tape and entered into the house. As soon as he saw the unzipped body bags, his knees got weak. He'd gotten the call that his mother, sister and nephew had been murdered. At the same time he received that message, Dymond had gotten the news about her mother, but she decided to stay back in Miami from fear of the authorities and even more so, Jock. Gunz was having none of that. He wanted to be sure it was his people before he went on a rampage. He fell to his knees right by his sister's body bag and opened it up, and as soon as he saw her face, he shook his head. He knew what it was and who it was. He kissed her on the forehead and did the same to the rest of the victims. He didn't even unzip his mother's bag all the way, because he didn't think he was strong enough to endure seeing her like that.

Later that night, he hopped in a Dodge Durango and rolled around Bankhead heavily armed, looking for Jock. Every nigga he thought looked like him caused him to slam on his brakes and lower his window, with his Mach .90 ready to spit, but he had not been so lucky. He tried Jock's phone, but the number was unable to receive calls. Gunz rolled around for three days straight in pursuit of him but couldn't locate him anywhere.

Everybody he asked said they had not seen him in a few days. That only pissed him off and made him want to kill something even worse. He wound up at the lakefront with his windows rolled up, shedding tears over his fallen loved ones. He knew they had paid for his sins, and it was eating at him worse than he ever imagined. He got out of his whip and slammed the door, after putting the forty-five on his hip. Gunz needed some fresh air, to allow the wind to beat against his face to dry his tears. He couldn't believe his mother and sister were gone. He never even got a fair chance to get to know Terrell. He'd promised more than once that he was going to pick the little boy up and take him to Disney World, but never followed through. Now he felt sick on the stomach with regrets.

The sun slowly set and brought on the night. Gunz sat on the hood of his Benz, and took a swallow of Patrón, reminiscing in his mind of all the good times he'd had with his sister. Their childhood and even the petty fights between them. He saw his mother's smiling face and then the body bag flashed into his mind. All four of them. He broke down again and tried to breathe, when a white Lexus pulled up alongside his whip. The car had mirror-tinted window and he could hear the trunk beating the sound of Yo Gotti's, "Rake It Up."

He jumped off his hood and straightened his Burberry button-up. The driver's side window rolled down slowly, before he saw a double barrel shotgun aimed at him and then the masked face of a man. "Turn them pockets inside out, my nigga and hurry up!"

Gunz froze in place. "What you say?" he asked, looking around to see the other people that were scattered around the parking lot running to their cars, slamming their doors and pulling off with smoke coming from under their tires.

"Nigga, I ain't gon' tell you no more," the masked gunman said through clenched teeth. "Turn yo pockets inside out, throw everything you got in this car and back the fuck up or I'm splashing you. Hurry up!" He cocked the shotgun and leveled it at Gunz's chest. Gunzs felt like panicking.

"Aiight chill, nigga. I got like two bands on me in my right pocket. You can have it, homie, all I care about is my life. This money ain't worth that."

"Nigga, shut yo bitch ass up and hurry the fuck up. Now!" the gunman lowered his eyes into slits. Gunz reached into his right pocket and felt the bundle of hundreds he had on him. He looked around the now deserted parking lot, before taking out all the bills and holding them in the air in his hand. "Where you want me to put it at? I know you don't want me to drop it on the ground, do you?" he asked, making his voice sound all whiny.

"Throw that shit in my window, right here," he said, letting down the back window. Gunz nodded.

"Aiight, bruh, just keep yo eyes on the money. I ain't trying shit funny." He moved the bundle from side to side in his hand and slowly walked to the back of the car. As soon as he got there, he dropped the cash on the back seat. The masked gunman went to point the shotgun toward him, but Gunz threw his big hand on the barrel of the gun and forced it downward.

Booom! It spit loudly into the night. The bullet hit the concrete and jumped into the air. Gunz continued to hold the barrel until it turned hot, burning him. Before he let go, he pulled the forty-five off his waist. "Let my shit go, bitch nigga and just run away. I ain't even fuckin wit you like that. I got what I wanted." *Booom*! The shotgun jumped again and spit a round right by Gunz's foot, slamming into his whip that was parked right next to the gunman's.

He took the forty-five and smacked the gunman in the face with it as hard as he could. The man jumped backward and fell into the passenger's seat, letting the shotgun fall on to the ground. He struggled and tried to get his glove box open, but Gunz was on his ass. He threw open the door and grabbed his leg, before placing the forty-five to his ass and pulling the trigger. *Boo-wa*! *Boo-wa*!

"Arrrgh! Shit. This nigga done shot me in my ass. Aww shit!" he hollered and flipped onto his stomach. Gunz got in the car and slammed the handle of his gun into his forehead, creating a bloody hole. He flipped it on safety, turned it around and slammed it into his forehead again and again, with blood shooting into the air. "Bitch. Nigga. You. Picked. The. Wrong. Day!" Gunz spat, beating him again and again, harder and harder.

He imagined his sister's face inside the body bag and his mother lying next to her. He thought about Terrell. It made him beat him harder and harder, until his arm was going so fast he was losing his breath. "Mommmaaaaa!" Gunz hollered. By the time he was done, the masked gunman's face was completely caved in. Blood leaked out of his eyes into the mask. Gunz elbowed him with all of his might, before getting out of the car and picking his money up from the backseat. He hated Atlanta and couldn't wait to break away from it. He promised himself that as soon as he buried his people and bodied Jock, he would never step foot in the city ever again.

* * *

"It ain't that I'm not happy to see you, it's just been a while and I thought you forgot about me. You know, ever since me and yo baby momma got into it last summer over you. I swear, I didn't know it was her responding to my messages. I would have never allowed for us to get caught up like that. That ain't even my style," Passion said, as she raised her Prada mini dress over her head and hung it up in her closet. She was five feet three inches tall, thick and as pretty as they came. Light-skinned, with small traces of freckles. Jock walked up to her from behind and rubbed his dick on her naked ass cheeks while she unhooked her bra in the front, allowing her yellow titties to spill out and into his hands. He bit her neck and sucked on it roughly.

"I heard y'all got cool after that. Kicking it and shit. Don't make it seem like y'all became enemies over me, because I already know what was really good." He reached around the front of her and put his hands between her legs, rubbing her bald pussy, before separating her lips and sliding a middle finger into her hotness. She moaned and stepped onto her tippy toes.

"Ummm, yeah. We was cool after that, once we got shit straight. She said she already knew you was out here doing yo thing, so it didn't bother her and since she knew me from school, she felt at least you had the decency to fuck wit' a bad bitch and not some tree monster. Gave me my props and I honored her slot. Told her I would never fuck around with' you at y'all's house and she was cool wit' that. When we kicked it, it was never about you. It was always about the shopping."

Jock grabbed a handful of her hair and pulled her back to him. She yelped and closed her eyes. Sometimes he way too rough, she was hoping it wasn't one of those times. As much as she missed him, she didn't feel like she was in the mood to be going through all of that. She had her son in his room down the hall, and she was sure he was up playing on his tablet. She didn't want him to hear them doing their thing. Besides, her baby daddy had just gotten home from the joint, and he was set to be back there in less than three hours. She knew she needed to get Jock into her and then right back out the door, which was his style anyway.

He never liked to stay around and cuddle. Usually after he spit his seed, he would be looking for the nearest exit or making her find one. Most times it got to her, but she was sure it wouldn't this time. He leaned down and bit into her neck, palming her breasts roughly, before suckling on her earlobe. "You know that bitch hit me for a lot of money and my daughter got hurt in the process of her betraying me. I been trying to find her ever since, but I'm having a hard time with that. I was wondering if you heard from her lately?" He pushed her to the bed.

She landed on her chest, before slowly turning around to face him. He took off his button-up and stood before her in just his boxers and black wife beater. He looked like he'd been taking steroids, the way his muscles were popped out. She had never seen him look so strong and ripped up. It was turning her on and making her terrified at the same time.

"The last time I talked to her was yesterday. She was saying something happened to her mother. She kept on breaking down, to the point I could barely understand what she was saying." Jock felt his heart skip a beat, and then get to pounding super hard in his chest. He could barely breathe. He pulled his boxers off, grabbed her hand and placed it on his dick. She started to stroke it right away, before scooting closer on the bed and popping it in her mouth, sucking him like a porn star. He closed his eyes and rested one of his big hands on her micro braids, while she darted her head back and forth. Out of all the women he had ever encountered, she was by far the best at giving head. She had a technique she did inside of her mouth that was second to none. It felt like she was sucking his soul out of him. He curled his toes and humped faster into her mouth, before pulling it all the way out. She made a loud sucking noise and her mouth was still going through the motions, before she opened her eyes and looked at him like he was crazy.

"You already know the routine, bend that ass over and spread them pussy lips for me, just like in high school," he said, stroking his dick up and down, waiting for her to assume the position.

Passion bit into her bottom lip, sucked on it for a few seconds, before getting on all fours, and laying her face on the bed. She spread her knees, reached under herself and opened her pussy lips wide, exposing her pink. " I miss that dick, Jock, I ain't gon' even lie. I want you to do me like you always do, but you gotta hurry up before Telly get home," she moaned, speaking in terms of her baby father. Jock rubbed his dick head up and down her wetness, before finding her hole, and slamming forward with force. "Uhhh! Shit, baby. Not so rough. Please just take it easy," she moaned with her eyes closed, already feeling her juices leak out of her.

Jock grabbed her hips and slammed her backward into him. Her hot pussy felt like she was still sucking his dick. He could feel her walls suffocating him, the scent of her pussy already in the air, mixed with the Prada perfume she'd made a habit of wearing ever since they were in high school. He made her lean all the way forward before pulling her back to him with aggression, then he started to beat her pussy in.

Passion moaned at the top of her lungs and their rhythm got to going. Jock was fucking her so fast she couldn't think straight. Long strokes that hit her bottom, before it pulled back, and hit it again. "Uhh! Shit! Jock, must you be so rough, baby? Damn, you be fucking me up down there. You gon' get me caught by my baby daddy, I swear you iz. Aww shit!" she screamed, forgetting about her son in the other room. Jock started to fuck her so hard he was hurting himself. He was trying to ruin her pussy. He saw Dymond's face in his mind and the hatred he had for her, so he started to take it out on Passion's box. The headboard got to beating into the wall so loud, it sounded like somebody was constantly slamming it into the wall on purpose. Jock clenched his teeth together and sped up the pace.

"Tell me where that bitch living at right now! Tell me, Passion!" he hollered, fucking her even harder. By this time, Passion had her eyes closed, with tears running down her cheeks. Her mouth was wide open as her face moved up and down on the mattress. He was hitting her deepest regions, and even though it was hurting her like a muthafucka, she couldn't deny it had her coming back-to-back. She could barely breathe. "I. I. I. don't know, Jock. Aww, shit! Aww! You killing me, baby. Please slow down," she groaned and buried her face into a pillow, biting it hard.

Jock smacked her on the ass hard and sped up his pace, taking a step forward, gripping her hips so hard his nails were cutting into them, causing her to bleed a little. "Where she staying at, Passion! Tell me, this shit ain't a game!" he hollered again through clenched teeth. Passion shook and came again. This was the third one and the fourth was already building. She couldn't understand why he was doing her like he was. It felt like he was deep within her stomach. She screamed into the pillow and bit it even harder. She tried to think where Dymond had told her she was as she felt him flip her over and force her knees to her chest, before slamming into her body again and going crazy with his long strokes. She felt his balls slamming into her ass. He bit into her neck so hard she just knew she was bleeding after he moved away to suck her titties.

"Tell me, bitch! Tell me right now! Arrggh!" He slammed into her over and over again, with hatred for Dymond. Passion threw the pillow against the wall and started to moan out loud. "Ah! Ah! Ah! Oh shit! Ah! Oh, my fucking Gawdddd! You're killing meeee!" Her body started to shake once again, so much she blacked out and came back to, screaming, "Miami. She in Miami. That bitch in Miami wit that nigga, Gunz. She told me don't say nothin, but fuck that! Fuck thaaat!" she hollered as she felt Jock releasing his seed, just as the door to her bedroom slammed open.

Chapter 12

Devin, aka Telly, stepped into the room with a baseball in his hands. "Bitch, I knew you wasn't right. I knew you had to be fuckin some nigga while I was on lock, and it's you." He choked up on the bat, to get as tight a grip as possible, before running over to the bed toward the pair. He lifted the bat in the air and brought it down against Jock's back. Jock fell to the carpet and winced in pain, before the next blow came, on the same spot. "Uhh! Bitch ass nigga!" He rolled to his stomach and watched as Devin dropped the bat and snatched Passion up by her throat. "You punk ass bitch. All that bullshit you told me while I was in there. Making it seem like you was so muthafucking one hunnit. You wait until I get out here, so you can do this type of shit?"

Passion's eyes got big as paper plates as she watched Jock stand up with an ugly mug on his face. He slammed the gun into the back of Devin's neck, causing his head to jerk forward. *Bloom! Bloom! Bloom!* "Bitch ass nigga!" Devin's neck exploded and his Adam's apple shot out and hit Passion in the forehead, before bouncing on the bed. Her entire face was covered in his blood and brain matter. She watched Devin slowly slump to the floor with his eyes wide open. She didn't even know she was screaming at the top of her lungs, until she felt Jock slam the gun down her throat so far that she threw up over the barrel. Jock pulled the trigger twice. *Bloom! Bloom!* Her insides exploded and she felt the hot pains in her stomach that eventually blew out her ass as she flew against the headboard. He looked down on her in disgust.

Jock hated conniving ass women. He felt if she could fuck him wit' her man being home, she was a trifling female all across the board. He got himself dressed and by the time he made it into her son's room, the little boy was trying to climb out of the second-story window with tears in his eyes. Jock jogged over to him and yanked him back into the room, throwing him to the floor. The little boy tried to get up and run. Jock closed one of his eyes and aimed. *Bloom*! *Bloom*! The little boy flew into the hallway, shaking and choking on his own blood. Jock came and stood over him. Imagining his daughter, her pretty face and the pain she must have felt as she was being murdered. He shook his head as large globs of blood poured out of the little boy's mouth. He coughed, before Jock finished him off with one shot to the face. *Bloom*!

* * *

"Now we got our backs against the wall and we're all we got, so y'all got to get an understanding, because this shit just got really real," Jahrome said, looking from Mami to Babygirl as they sat on the bed in their motel room, looking up at him as if every word due to come out of his mouth had the power of life and death in it.

Mami got up and took a deep breath. "Look, people are steady dying in my family right and left. Things are getting real for me too, and I'd like to think that you guys are my true family now." She turned to Babygirl, who sat there looking at the floor. "Look, I'm not trying to steal your brother away from you. I would never set out to do that. But I do love him, and I am his woman. I don't understand why it's so hard for you to accept that."

Babygirl looked at her with hatred. She still wasn't over the fact that Mami had knocked her out. She just couldn't wrap her head around the prospect of being cool with her. Deep in the pits of her mind, she was thinking of a way she could kill the woman and get away with it. She didn't feel like she would ever change her mind, she hated her. Babygirl wanted

Jahrome for herself and she didn't care what the world said about it. He was her everything and she had to have him. Alone. "That's the thing. It ain't about me understanding you're his woman, I get all of that. It's just that you want to be the one he loves the most. You're so fucking needy." She looked up at her with the look of death.

"Out of the both of us, I'm the needy one? Really are you fucking kidding me right now?" Mami laughed sarcastically. "You're the one that's always under him for one reason or the next, so much so that it's like you're more his woman than his sister. I don't get it."

Babygirl was over her. "Bitch, what don't you get?" she said, hopping off of the bed and walking toward her with both fists balled.

Mami took a step back and slowly balled up her own fists. "Look, Jahrome, you better get her. I'm not kidding either." She pointed at her and shook her head slowly, tired of her bullshit already.

Jahrome jumped up and grabbed Babygirl, wrapping his arms around her, kissing the back of her neck. "Calm down, ma. It's okay, Babygirl. Ain't no reason for you to feel how you feeling right now because there is no threat to you, you hear me?" She felt his huge muscles wrapped around her and she immediately softened. In her book, there was nothing like the feeling of being in his arms. It made her feel so loved and safe. It was all she felt she needed and would ever need. She never wanted to share him and that was that.

Mami saw the way Babygirl's whole demeanor changed and it made her so jealous. She was starting to really dislike the needy woman. She felt something wasn't right between her and Jahrome, she was missing about the pair that she couldn't quite put her finger on.

Babygirl took a deep breath and slowly blew it out. "Mami, just let me get an understanding with my brother for a minute and the next time you and I talk, I'll be ready to squash this beef stuff between us. I give you my word on that."

Mami nodded. "So what, you want me to go into the bathroom or something while y'all talk, or y'all gon' step in there, what?"

Babygirl nodded. "Would you please? I just wanna nip this shit in the bud, that's all."

"And you can't do that with me standing right here?" Mami asked, frowning.

Jahrome held up a hand. "Babygirl, what's good? Why she gotta leave the room and shit?" Babygirl turned around and looked into his eyes.

"Because I just need to ask you a few questions, because I'm thinking about leaving y'all alone and letting y'all live yo lives. But before I do that, I just need a few things clarified. Am I asking too much?"

Mami heard she was getting ready to leave and damn near broke her neck getting out of the room. "N'all, you know what, if you need to do that then I'll step out. I mean, it ain't my business anyway." She walked over to Jahrome and kissed him on the cheek. "Hear her out, Papi and give her the best possible advice."

Babygirl waited until she was in the bathroom with the door closed, before she grabbed Jahrome's arm and pulled him to the side, then pushed his back against the wall before leaning in and kissing him on the lips. She breathed into his face with her eyes closed and sucked on his lips, wrapping her arms around the top of his neck, looking into his hazel eyes. "I just need to know one thing, and I want you to be honest wit' me about it too."

Jahrome looked toward the bathroom door and prayed it didn't open. He put his finger to Babygirl's lips, letting her know to speak a little lower. "What's that?" he asked, barely above a whisper. She reached between them and slid her hand down into his pants and boxers, grabbing his dick and holding it.

"I need to know if I submit to this bitch being yo woman, and I take a step back and allow for y'all to do all that lovey-dovey shit all the time, that I'm still gon' get some of this whenever I want it. Which will be a lot?" she asked, kissing his neck. Jahrome couldn't stop his piece from rising in her hand. It had a mind of its own, it didn't help that she was running her thumb back and forth across his big head. He closed his eyes when he felt her squeeze him.

She bit into his neck and sucked hard. "Umm. Tell me, lil' bruh. Tell me this gon' belong to me just as much as it will her." She stroked him inside his boxers and moaned into his ear. He opened his eyes and peeked at the bathroom door. He could only imagine what Mami would say if she caught Babygirl's hand down his pants. He wanted to pull it out so bad, but the way she was working his head was driving him crazy. She used to the do the same thing to him when he was little. He bit into his bottom lip.

"Yeah, ain't shit gon' change between me and you Babygirl, you should already know that." He closed his eyes again and allowed her to do her thing for a minute before his common sense kicked in and he pulled her hand out of his pants. He took a step back and held her by her shoulders. "Look sis, we gotta get on some grown shit. I love you and you know we gon' do our thing together, but I can't allow for that to rule my whole life. I think what it's gon' take is for you honestly, is to find somebody to love you the way Mami love me."

Babygirl felt her heart beating fast in her chest. It felt like she was about to pass out. She couldn't believe he would say something like that to her. She couldn't understand why he didn't feel the same way she did. Why he wasn't naturally crazy about her the way she was for her? She felt sick to her stomach and before she could stop herself, she pushed him out of her face and lowered her head.

Jahrome stumbled backward a couple paces and caught his footing. "What the fuck is wrong wit' you, sis?"

Babygirl stood there for a long time with her head bowed, shaking it slowly from right to left. "Damn, Jahrome." She blinked back tears and felt like her heart had been ripped out of her chest. She balled up her fists and felt so angry, she couldn't see straight. Jahrome tried to walk over to her, but she pushed him away again, this time with so much force that he wanted to snap the fuck out and chastise her.

Babygirl had never felt as low as she felt in that moment. His last comments kept on replaying themselves over and over again in her mind. She felt like a schoolgirl that had lost her virginity to a boy that dumped her as soon as he came. She looked up to him with a heart torn in two. "You gon' make me kill that girl, huh?" She nodded her head. "Yeah, that's just what I gotta do. That's the only way you gon' get it through yo head that you and I are supposed to be together." She walked past him and ran to the bed, throwing the pillow on the floor that his gun was under, before picking up the gun and cocking it back. "I gotta kill this bitch because you're mine, Jahrome." Tears ran down her cheeks and dripped off of her chin. Her nose ran and she didn't even care, all she cared about was him, and killing the woman inside of the bathroom.

Jahrome bucked his eyes and took a step back with his hands in the air. "Babygirl, get off that dumb shit. You're bugging right now. Give me that nine before you hurt yourself fucking wit' it."

She shook her head, deep in her own zone. She couldn't see straight, she felt like she was under a dark cloud, like she was having an out-of-body experience. Her heart hurt too bad for anything to make sense. She raised the gun and pointed it at him. "Jahrome, I love you. But if you try and stop me from killing this bitch, I'm gon' kill you, her and then myself, because I'm not living in this world without you. Now, I need you all to myself and you don't get that, because this bitch is breathing. Once I whack her ass, then you will. So, step back!" she screamed, as Mami came out of the bathroom to see what all of the racket was about.

As soon as she saw Babygirl pointing the gun at Jahrome, she ran over and stood in front of him with her eyes closed. "Babygirl, please don't do this. Don't kill yo brother. I need him so, so bad. Please. Whatever the problem is, I promise we can all work it out." She scrunched her face and prepared for the impact of the bullets.

Jahrome put her behind him and stood in front of her protectively. He refused to allow anything to happen to her. It was his job to protect her and he knew he would at all costs. "Babygirl, give me the fucking gun and get off this dumb shit! Now!"

She backed up, crying, shaking her head from right to left. "You know what, Jahrome? I see you really love that girl. I can see it all in your eyes. She means the world to you and that's killing me. I don't have nobody no more because she stole you. I don't have no mother, no father. Now I ain't got no brother and don't nobody want me. This world is too painful, and I can't take this shit no more." She put the gun in her mouth and put her finger on the trigger, pulling it with all her might.

"Nooo!" Jahrome ran to her at full speed as she took it out of her mouth, saw that it was on safety, flipped the switch and got ready to put it back in there. He dived, tackling her to the floor as the gun went off. *Boom*! Mami felt the searing pain as the bullet slammed into her stomach and knocked her backward. She fell on her back as the blood poured out of her gut and everything faded to black.

Chapter 13

"That's that bitch ass spic right there. I told you, it's every Saturday like clockwork," Ross said as he lowered the Tom Ford glasses on his nose. "Another important rule to this game, lil' cuz, is that you should never allow your habits to become so mechanical that a nigga be able to read you and know when and how you're going to make yo next move. Once you get too routine, shit get dangerous and you'll be the muthafucka that get they head knocked off like this nigga fin to do."

Gunz nodded and pulled down his ski mask. "What about them?" he asked, pointing at the two bodyguards that walked behind Santiago as if they were about to stop his murder from happening. He watched the three of them walk up the driveway to the brick house, then Santiago reached under the flowerpot and entered the house, leaving his two goons to stand guard at the door. Through the window, Gunz could see a white girl run into his arms and wrap her legs around him. Ross smiled and looked through the back window of their Benz to see if anybody else was out and about in the dark residential neighborhood. He screwed the silencer onto his forty-five and watched as Gunz did the same thing to his as well. "The boss don't usually like to get his hands dirty, but I'll make an exception for this bitch nigga."

He tapped his finger on the trigger to make sure the red beam would be enacted. When the red glow shone from the top of his gun, he smiled. The sun was just beginning to set. He waited until Santiago stepped into the town home and closed the door. From a few cars down the street, he could see Santiago's bodyguards come and stand in front of the door blocking it as if they were Secret Servicemen. Ross wasn't worried about none of that. He lowered his ski mask, and softly opened the door to his whip. He stepped into the night, with a calm feeling breezing over him. "Gunz, you stay right here. Just watch me in action. I'll show you all of that money ain't changed a nigga." He closed the door and crept through the yard of the house they were parked in front of, ran alongside of it, and down the back alley. When he got to the gate of Santiago's town home, he hopped it and ran across the backyard. In seconds, he crept beside the porch where the security men were set up. He could smell their musky cologne.

Ross took a deep breath, and side stepped over and over until he could properly aim his gun. Then he took his time and lined the beam up with the first bodyguard's temple. When he was sure he was locked in, he pulled the trigger twice. The first bodyguard's head splattered, and he fell over the railing. His partner was confused. He rushed over to see what the hell had happened. Ross hopped on to the porch and knelt on one knee. He closed his right eye and aimed, lining the beam up with the back of his head, then squeezed the trigger back-to-back, stunning the second bodyguard, and taking his life immediately. He walked up on him and waved Gunz over.

Gunz jogged until he got up on the porch. He'd watched Ross in action and couldn't help but to be fascinated by how easily the man had taken out two men. It was impressive to him, to say the least. "Now what?" he whispered, close to Ross.

Ross grabbed the key from the fallen guard's waistband and entered it in the lock, turned it and pushed the door inward. "Now we find his bitch ass and handle this bidness," Ross whispered. He sniffed the air. There was a heavy scent of sex. He smiled again. "Shit gon' be a piece of cake."

Gunz stepped in beside him. The first thing he smelled was the sex in the air. He could hear the sounds of Frank Sinatra playing upstairs. Ross led the way up the stairs with his gun held it out in front of him. When he got to the top flight, he paused and held his breath. In doing so, he was able to hear grunting and moaning over the music. The scent of pussy was louder than ever now. He slowly crept down the hall until he was standing in front of Santiago's room. He placed his ear to the door and listened. Once he confirmed they were still in there screwing, he eased open the door and stepped into the room.

Santiago had Amanda on top of his waist, riding away. She held his shoulders and bounced up and down on his manhood. Tossed her head back and screaming as if he were killing her in the worst way, though it was all an act. In her opinion Santiago could barely scratch the surface of her itch, but it was in her best interest to fake it until she made it. Sleeping with the drug lord had its many perks. He kept her in top notch everything, and with his prestige, she was able to moonlight with the upper crust. She continued to ride him fast and hard. "Un. Un. Yeah, baby. Yes!" she groaned.

Ross stepped to the side of the bed and pinned his red beam right on Santiago's forehead. "How 'bout you get yo punk ass out of the pussy for a minute?"

Amanda's eyes got as big as saucers. Before she could scream, Gunz wrapped his hand around her mouth and yanked her from the bed. Then he wrapped his arm around her neck and proceeded to choke her out as hard as he could. He could feel her bones cracking under the pressure he was applying.

Ross grabbed Santiago by the neck and yanked him from the bed so fast, Santiago's toupee flew off his sweaty scalp. He was flung to the ground. Ross placed his knee in his chest. "Muthafucka, I told you Miami was mine. Any muthafucka that think they gone stand in my way, gone feel the wrath of a boss. Look at yo bitch ass, you're pathetic. I'll never wind up like you."

Santiago scooted backward and bumped into the bed. He closed his eyes still in disbelief. "I'll make you a rich man. Spare me. Just name your price. Anything you want is yours. Just spare me."

Ross pulled his mask off and looked Santiago right in the eyes. "I don't want shit from you. Rest in hell, Santiago." Ross finger-fucked his trigger back-to-back, filling the man with hole after hole.

Gunz dropped Amanda and stepped over her. "Come on, you ready to get up out of here?"

Ross mugged Santiago for a second longer, already knowing what his death meant. With Santiago wiped out, it meant he would be able to fully take over the reins of Miami. The port would be his to get filthy rich off of. He couldn't help cheesing. "Yeah, cuz, let's get the fuck up out of here."

Chapter 14

"Arrrgh! Arrrgh! Jock, what the fuck! I never came at you bogus! Come on, man! This shit ain't cool!" Clod hollered as Jock ran the blade from the top of his forehead, all the way down his face, past his chest and to his stomach, before slamming it into his shoulder with all of his might. Clod was stretched out on the counter of Bam-Bam's Lounge, after making a drop off to the owner. Jock caught Bam-Bam just as he opened the doors and put the forty-five to his head, walked him right into his establishment and told him what it was. That if he complied, he'd let him leave with his life, but if he did anything out of the ordinary, he would kill him and still handle the drop off from the Haitians. So, after they got an understanding, he knelt behind the bar with the gun pressed to Bam-Bam's nuts, until Clod entered the lounge with the suitcase full of heroin. As soon as he was fully inside, Jock stood up and pointed the gun at him until he was close enough. Then he wrapped his arm around his neck and made Bam-Bam tie him up. Now as it stood, he was laid across the bar, with Jock handling his business.

Clod hollered and it made Jock smile. He turned around and pressed the barrel of his forty-five to Bam-Bam's forehead and, *Boom*! *Boom*! He pulled the trigger, splattering his brains all over the liquor bottles behind him. Bam-Bam fell to the floor brainless, his eyes wide open. Jock kicked him away from him and turned back to Clod. It was seven at night and the hood was used to Bam-Bam's opening at around ten, which meant he had three hours to do his business, but he didn't plan on using more than twenty minutes.

He put his pistol back on his hip and picked up the steak knife, slamming it into Clod's left shoulder so hard it went through him and pierced the wood up under Clod. "Arrrgh!

Jock! Please! What have I done to you? Why are you doing this to me?" Jock twisted the knife in his shoulder, causing him to scream like a female.

"Tell me who Marvey got looking for me? How much money he got on my head? Huh?"

Clod was out of breath. The pain hurt so bad he was seeing two of Jock. "He got five hundred thousand on yo head, Jock, but he want you alive. The price tag goes down to two hundred thousand if anybody kill you first. He say he want to personally cut off yo head himself. That if anybody denies him of that great pleasure, they gon' pay for it."

He felt Jock snatch the knife out of his shoulder and wipe the blade clean on his clothes. He raised it over his head and slammed it into his thigh, twisting it with all of his might. Clod could feel the tendons in his thighs snapping, his muscle opening up wide. "Jock! What the fuck you want from me? I'm answering yo every question, man, please stop this shit!" He cried real tears.

Jock grabbed a bottle of Hennessy from the bar and took off the cap, placing it into his pocket, before taking long swallows of the alcohol. He burped and wiped his mouth. "Where the fuck he stay in Florida? I want this bitch nigga's address. I mean, any place he could be at. I want that shit and I want it now. Keep in mind that he my fucking uncle, so I already know a lot. You try to do anything stupid and I'm gon' torture you for the next three hours and I'm gone have some fun, because I hate you Haitian muthafuckas wit' a passion."

Clod tried to sit up, with tears running out of his eyes. Blood leaked down his cheeks and all over his body. His dreads were caked in it. It looked like somebody took a pot of spaghetti sauce and poured it over his head. "I can't tell you where he stay, Jock. That fool would kill me. He'd know it came straight from my mouth. He would kill everybody that

I. Arrrghhh!" Jock slammed the steak knife into the right side of his chest and ripped it downward. Blood spurted up and shot across his arm.

He slashed him across the face ten times and slammed him back on to the bar. "Nigga, and you think I won't?" He took the steak knife, slammed it into his lower abdomen and sliced it open, taking four fingers on each side ripping the hole as far open as he could. He could hear Clod's skin tearing.

"Arrrgh! Okay! Oh-muthafucking kay! Fuck, I can't take this shit. I can't take this shit no more." He started to holler out every address he thought Marvey would be at. He even gave him the addresses to his kids'. Jock logged everything into his new phone and took Clod's and drained it of information, before turning it off and putting it into his pocket. He would dispose of it at his earliest convenience. Jock took another long swallow from the bottle of Hennessy, before setting it on the bar a little ways down. He looked at Clod with hatred.

"I hate snitches like you. Y'all make this game too easy for bitch niggas to survive in. All the weight should have been on my shoulders to find Marvey, but yo bitch ass gave me everything I needed. That's fuck shit. This nigga done kept you fed, got you driving a Range Rover, and put food on yo family's table. You's a bitch!" He imagined that Clod was Gunz and he developed a deeper hatred for him. He took the knife, raised it over his head and slammed it into Clod's face with all of his might. The blade landed in one of his eyes, popping it immediately. Blood gushed out of it right away. He pulled the knife back and slammed it into his face again, not noticing Clod's eye was stuck to it. The blade sliced through his facial meat. "Arrrgh! Help me! Help me!" Clod screamed, gurgling on his own blood. Before it was all said and done, Jock stabbed him over fifty times in the face again and again, imagining him being his double-crossing ex right-hand man, Gunz.

* * *

"Mami! Mami! Baby, wake up. Are you okay?" Jahrome asked, leaning over and kissing her on the forehead. They had taken the bullet out of her more than two hours ago and she had still not awakened. That scared Jahrome to death, even though the doctor told him she was well into recovery mode. The bullet had not pierced any vital organs. She was blessed to say the least. Babygirl paced back and forth in the room. She was nervous and didn't know what to do or how to behave. She hadn't meant to shoot Mami, but she had. Now she was laying in the hospital bed and they'd had to tell the local authorities someone had tried to rob her. The police had stated after their questioning they would need to get Mami's side of the story when she woke up, and that spooked Babygirl, because she didn't know what the girl was going to say. She just hoped and prayed she didn't tell on her. It would have been the easiest way for Mami to get rid of her indefinitely. Babygirl didn't know if she herself wouldn't have cashed in on that opportunity to get rid of her.

Jahrome leaned down and kissed her soft cheek, before nuzzling his face into her. It was warm and she smelled like alcohol pads. The little breathing device that went into her nose was freaking him out. He needed to see her eyes open up. "Baby, wake up for me, please." He kissed her forehead again.

Mami's eyes fluttered and then they opened. She blinked, closed them back, before opening them wide. She tried to speak but her throat was so dry, it was preventing her from doing so. She coughed and sat up in bed, with her eyes bugged out of her head.

Babygirl ran over to the bed after poking the straw through the top of the juice box. She got to Mami's side and placed the straw to her lips, allowing her to suck the juice up through it. She looked at Jahrome and rolled her eyes. "Damn, didn't you peep what was wrong?"

He shook his head, looking down on Mami. "Baby, are you okay?" She swallowed the juice in small increments, before slowly nodding her head. "Why did you let her shoot me, Jahrome? I thought you were my protector?" she asked in a raspy voice. Jahrome lowered his head, while Babygirl slowly backed away from the bed with the juice in her hand.

"I ain't do that shit on purpose, Mami. I was trying to kill myself. He just got in the way."

Mami blinked and winced in pain as her stomach started to ache where they'd pulled the bullet out of her. "Uh! Well, you did a poor job because the bullet that was supposed to hit you got me. I don't know why you hate me so much, Babygirl. I've never done anything to you, besides defended myself while you tried to attack me for no reason. I've never had a man's sister hate me for loving her brother. So, what gives?" She winced in pain again.

Jahrome kissed her on the forehead and rubbed her soft cheek. "Baby, we gon' have to talk about that later, because as soon as the nurses know you're awake, they're supposed to alert the authorities so they can question you about the shooting. I told them it was a botched robbery and you gotta stick to that script. That's important."

Mami nodded. "Okay, Papi, that's no problem. But I still want to know why does she hate me so much?" Just as she asked him that question, the door opened, and the doctor stepped into the room. She was a short East Indian woman, with a red dot on her forehead.

"How goes it, Ms. Jimenez? How are you feeling, my darling?" She walked over to the monitors and started to check her vitals. Jahrome stepped out of the way and stood beside Babygirl. She wrapped her arm around his waist and laid her head on his shoulder.

Mami peeped it out the corners of her eyes and felt sick all over again. "I'm doing okay, my tummy hurts a little bit. Is that normal?" She adjusted herself in the bed. "Oh, and I feel sick on the stomach, like I want to throw up every few seconds."

The doctor frowned. "Well, you're fresh out of surgery so the pain is normal. The sickness could be attributed to the fact that you're pregnant." She continued to check over the monitors as if she hadn't just dropped a bombshell on them all.

Mami swallowed and felt ten times sicker. "What do you mean, pregnant?"

The doctor stopped and looked her over closely and gave her a look that said she didn't know Mami was unaware of being pregnant. "Wait, so you really didn't know? Oh, I'm sorry. I didn't know that."

Babygirl felt her knees get wobbly. She fell against Jahrome, who held her up and led her to the couch where he sat her down. She grew instantly dizzy and could barely breathe. She felt like her life was over and once again, she was back to having strong thoughts of killing Mami. This time she knew she was going to really kill her. There was no way possible she was going to allow her to have his baby. Babygirl didn't feel like she was strong enough to endure that.

She felt sick because there was an image going through her head of Mami having Jahrome's baby, and Babygirl being left out in the cold to fend for herself. Once that baby arrived, she just knew her brother wouldn't have any more time for her. He would surely kick her to the curb and be all about his little family. She felt like screaming. She had to kill Mami, there was no way around it she felt. After Jahrome led her to the couch and sat her down, he rushed to the bed to stand beside Mami. He placed his hand on her forehead and looked deep into her eyes. She looked worried and severely confused.

"But, I don't understand, Doctor. So, you're saying inside of my body right now is a baby and it's going to be born through me?" She knew her question made no sense, but nothing the doctor had told her thus far made sense to her. She didn't know if she was ready to have a baby, didn't know if she was strong enough to push an entire child out of her womb. She didn't know where she stood with Jahrome and what role Babygirl played in the grand scheme of all of it. She had so many questions that needed to be answered, before she even thought she was part-way ready to be a mother to his child. For as long as she could remember, her body had been what paid the bills and she wondered how much a baby would cause her to lose. The women in her family had a tendency to gain a little weight during their pregnancies, and it was hell getting it back off.

She feared if she wasn't able to make some sort of financial contribution, Jahrome would wind up leaving her for good and that worried her, because now that her brother was gone and her cousin was constantly under the gun, she felt she really didn't have anybody.

The doctor looked down on her and smiled. She grabbed her hand and rubbed the back of it with her thumb. "Well, you are very pregnant and very healthy. That little hole we patched up won't hurt your child one bit. You're going to be just fine, mark my words." She grabbed her clipboard and left the room, closing the door behind her.

Mami sat all the way up in the bed and put her face into her hands. "This just can't be happening. This isn't true. Somebody please tell me I didn't get shot and find out I'm pregnant, all in one day. What am I going to do?" She slammed both of her fists on the bed and threw her head back on the pillow.

Jahrome frowned. "What you mean, what are you going to do? You ain't in this alone. I got you one hundred percent and our child that's growing inside of your stomach." He tried to grab her hand, but she yanked it away from him before wincing in pain. She closed her eyes and struggled to breathe. "Aw, this shit hurts so fucking bad," she said, placing her hand under the covers, on her stomach wound.

Jahrome moved her long hair away from her face and looked her over closely. "Baby, you do know I got you, right? I mean, you gotta know I'ma hold you down the way I'm supposed to." He rubbed her soft cheek, before kissing it lightly. Mami shook her head. She didn't know what to do or think and it was killing her, because she didn't know if she believed him or not. It had nothing to do with her thinking he wasn't stand-up or anything like that, she felt he had a weakness for his sister that was sure to stand in the way of their family and relationship. She didn't know how much more she could take, being inside the crazy love triangle. Before she found out she was pregnant, she was really having second thoughts about them being together, period. She blinked back tears.

"Jahrome, you can't even control and take care of yo sister without me being hurt. You think I want to bring a baby into this equation? How smart would that be?" she asked dryly.

Jahrome stood straight up, with his face scrunched. "So what, you thinking about killing our child or something?" he asked, ready to snap. There was no way he was going to allow that to happen. He would just ask her for full custody first and raise their kid on his own. He couldn't understand why she was being so stubborn and negative. To him, everything that had taken place before they found out she was pregnant mattered, but then again it didn't, because a baby was supposed to change everything.

Mami shook her head. "N'all, I'm not saying I want to do anything just yet. I think we have a lot of talking to do, but we damn sure can't avoid the elephant in the room." She paused, before looking over at Babygirl. Babygirl sat on the couch with her head down, looking at the floor. She was lost deep within her mind, trying to imagine what life would look like without her brother. All her visions kept doing was making her sicker and sicker. She heard Mami's last comment, and it snapped her back to reality. She stood up.

"Here you go again, attacking me. I don't have anything to do with you being pregnant, yet you're going to make it out to be my fault, or like I'm the problem. Well, I'm tired of all that shit, Mami. I'm tired of always feeling like the villain whenever I am around you. So, you know what? I'ma go about my business and figure things out on my own, and you can have my brother. You just better take good care of him and that one growing inside of your stomach, because if you don't, then we gon' have some serious problems."

Mami looked at her for a long time, before rolling her eyes. "So, when are you leaving, because the sooner the better. You been saying it for how long now?" She laughed. "When does it become a reality?"

Babygirl looked at Jahrome and all he did was lower his head in silence. She felt hurt and a little trapped, like she was being called out on her bullshit, and she didn't know what to do or say. She fought back tears. "When we get back to the motel, I'ma just get my shit and figure it out. It's cool, I want y'all to be happy." She slowly walked toward the door. "I'll be waiting for you in the car." Then she walked out the door and left, headed to the parking lot.

Jahrome was on his way to catch up with her because he didn't want her to do anything stupid, when Mami started laughing. It caused him to pause in his tracks and turn around to face her.

"You see, that's what I mean, Jahrome. Every time she cry or moan, you gotta be the one to rescue her like you're her Superman or something. When will you allow her to grow up and become a woman? After all, you're younger than she is."

Jahrome took a deep breath and looked back over his shoulder toward the open door. He had a vision of his sister running away and something bad happening to her. He didn't want that on his conscience. He had already dropped the ball one time and because he had, she had almost been killed and now walked around with a scar across her face that was a constant reminder of what had taken place.

He didn't think Mami fully understood all they had been through together, and he didn't have the time to explain it all to her. He walked over to the bed and took her hand. "Look, Mami. Like I said before, I love you and I'ma hold you down to the best of my ability. I wanna be wit' you, and I'll never let nobody take yo place as my woman, contrary to how you may be feeling right now." He paused and knelt down beside her. "Babygirl is my sister and I love her as well. I'm all she has right now, and it's because I already failed her once, and our mother. You have no idea how much that shit kills me every single day. Every time I see that scar across her face, it's a constant reminder of how I failed her." He shook his head and held her hand firmer. "I ain't like other niggas. I got a little heart for my people. I feel like it's my job to protect them from this cold ass world to the best of my abilities. So, when I fail at that task, I feel like less than a man. Every time I see that scar across her face, that's exactly how I feel."

Ghost

Chapter 15

Babygirl reached under Jahrome's driver's seat and grabbed the nine millimeter, with tears streaming down her cheeks. "I'm so sorry, Momma, but I gotta kill this girl. I gotta kill her, Momma. Please forgive me, because after I kill her, I'm bringing me and Jahrome home to you too." Babygirl rocked back and forth in the car for a full ten minutes, before jumping out, with murder on her mind. There nothing that was going to stop her from killing Mami.

* * *

Mami wrapped her arms around Jahrome even tighter, laying her head on his chest. "Baby, I understand that you're different from other men, because of how you view the world. I'm not holding that against you. How could I, as a woman? All I'm saying is there comes a time when you have to step a few paces back, so she can figure life out a little bit. Your mother's death was not yo fault. Reggie attacking Babygirl was not yo fault. You did what you could, and things turned out how they did. You are not to blame." She hugged him tighter. "I just need to know you're going to be there for us, Papi. I need to know we will become your priority. That you will love us as hard as you love your sister and mother." Jahrome swallowed and slowly nodded his head. He understood where she was corning from and felt she had the right to be concerned, as a woman bringing a child into their world. Now that she was pregnant, she had to become his priority. Her and their child. He would never turn his back on Babygirl, but she would have to understand his new position as a father.

"Baby, I promise you are my first priority, and our child will be as well. I'm gone need you to help guide me at times, so I stay on course, but on my Mom's in heaven, I'ma hold you down first and foremost."

* * *

Babygirl took the nine off her waist and threw open the door to Mami's room with tears in her eyes. Before she could allow herself to lose her nerve, she aimed at the woman and started shooting.

* * *

"Surprise-surprise, muthafucka!" Ross hollered, slamming the banger into the back of Sanchez's head. He watched Sanchez fall on the side of Cassy. Sanchez tried to jump up, Ross smacked him again with the .40 caliber. Gunz picked the fallen man up by the throat and placed him in a full nelson, standing him up on the side of the bed.

Sanchez hollered out in pain as he felt the blood running down the back of his neck. He could hear Gunz's heavy breaths at the back of his head. Gunz tightened his hold and held the man off his feet.

Cassy stood up and walked over to Ross, rubbing his chest. "Hey daddy, 'bout time you got here. The son of a bitch had the nerve to fuck me without protection, even after I begged him to use some. He deserves everything he got coming to him. I hope you kill him like his dope did my sister last summer," the strawberry blonde said, sliding her naked body into her robe.

Ross smiled and nodded his head. "I'll tell you what, baby girl, since you're feeling some type of way I'll let you take first stab at it." He opened his jacket and pulled a Kitana from his inside coat pocket. The knife had been concealed in a leather sheath. "How does that sound?"

Cassy backed up and shook her head. "I don't know about that, Ross. I mean, I ain't never killed nobody before. I wouldn't know the first thing about doing any such thing."

Sanchez struggled against Gunz. "Get your filthy monkey hands off me, you gorilla. You're gonna allow some coke whore to kill me, Ross? Huh? After all I've done for you?" Sweat slid down the side of his swollen face. "What's the matter, you too pussy to do it yourself?"

Ross busted up laughing. "Oh the contrary, muthafucka. I wouldn't hesitate to slice and dice yo ass. But, seeing as your product took the life of her sister, I think it's only right that she's allowed a little revenge. Wouldn't you agree, Cassy?"

Cassy started to shake. "I'm scared, Ross. I'm not gon' even lie. I'm scared out of my fuckin mind." She was even more afraid to make eye contact with Ross. She didn't know how he was going to take the news.

"I'll do it, cuz. You said once I hit this racist muthafucka, you was gon' give me the keys to the empire. Well I'm ready to hit his ass right now. I'll snap his neck like a twig, and we can get this shit over right now, if need be. Just tell me what you want me to do." Gunz's heartbeat sped up. He was ready to be done with Sanchez.

Ross shook his head. "N'all, before you do anything, she gon' put some of this stainless steel to his ass. Ain't no muthafuckin way she think we finna walk out or here without doing something. That ain't how the game go, and this bitch know it. Cassy, get yo ass over here and grab this blade. I want you to make incisions on his ass like he in surgery or something." Ross reached out for her.

Cassy backed up once again. Now she was against the door with her ass and back pressed against it. "Why can't you just do it, Ross? I don't think I'd ever be able to live with myself if I did it. I'm just not strong enough."

Sanchez tried to slump down using all of his weight. Gunz picked him up into the air and tightened his full nelson. "The more you try and fight with me, muthafucka, the tighter this hold is going to get. It's best you stay yo punk ass real still or shit ain't gon' do nothing but get worse for you."

Sanchez twisted and felt the undeniable pain in his arms, and face. "This is bullshit, Ross. This is some coward shit and you know it. I would have never come for you like this. You have no idea how many times I could have taken your life, and I allowed you to live. Show me the same fuckin decency. Have some honor about yourself, you no-good scum bag," Sanchez spat.

Ross grabbed Cassy by her robe and pulled her to him. He looked directly into her eyes. "Cassy, listen to me, lil' one. It's only one way up out of this house tonight, and this Columbian is your ticket. Now, I don't know what you're going to have to envision, or what must go through your mind, but you're not leaving here until you take this Kitana and you poke his ass up like a pin cushion. Do you understand me?"

She nodded and blinked tears. "Okay, just tell me what to do, and where to stab. I swear, I don't know how to do any of these things." She kept her gaze fixed on the floor.

Ross placed his arm around her neck. "How about we start with your sister's name? Tell me, what was her name?"

"Her name was Mary." Cassy began to imagine her sister in her mind's eye.

"And were you and Mary close?" Ross asked, stepping behind her and placing his lips on her ear.

Cassy nodded. "Before her drug use, she was my best friend. We did everything together. We were inseparable." Her voice began to crack.

"And let me guess," Ross whispered, "when she overdosed off of Sanchez's product, it shattered you?"

"For sure. My brain has been fucked up ever since. She told me he purposely got her hooked on that shit. That was the only way he could turn her into a full-time call girl. She was only sixteen years old when he first got ahold of her. He ruined my sister."

Ross slid the Kitana into her hand and kissed her neck. "It's okay, baby. It's okay. That's why daddy here. Daddy gone make sure this ma'fucka pay for what he did to Mary, but you gon' have to help me. There ain't no free lunches here, goddess. Ask him why he did it. Ask him. He'll tell you why he turned your sister out with no remorse and forced her to sell her body, before she ultimately overdosed off his product. A product he made purposely strong to keep her hooked. Ask him!" Ross hollered.

Cassy jumped. "Why did you do it, Sanchez? What would possess you to turn out a kid?" Her bottom lip quivered as she held the knife in her right hand. "Answer me!"

Sanchez scoffed. "Mary was a born whore. She came to me with legs wide open, begging for my sausage. After a few lays, she refused to go home and since she refused, I told her in order to stay in my presence she had to earn her way. The habit she picked up along the way."

"But why didn't you send her home? She was only sixteen. You should have never allowed her to get involved with you. You are nothing more than a monster!" she screamed, stepping forward.

Sanchez laughed. "I'm the monster? You ungrateful bitch, I took care of Mary for three whole years, and this is the thanks

I get? I helped her pay your meth addict mother's bills on more than one occasion, so you can kiss my ass. As far as I'm concerned, life goes on. The bitch is dead."

"It's your fault." Cassy raised the Kitana over her head and brought it down into his left shoulder. The feel of the steel cutting through his muscles and tissue freaked her out. She left the blade inside him and backed all the way up, before slumping to the ground.

Sanchez closed his eyes and refused to cry out from the pain. When he opened them, Gunz yanked the Kitana blade out and he flung Sanchez into the wall. "I got this shit, Ross. That empire is mine." He rushed him like a raging bull, swinging both his fist and the Kitana. The attack happened so fast, Sanchez was delayed in protecting himself. First, he'd feel a punch and then a stab. In a matter of minutes, he was bleeding all over the floor. Sanchez fell to his knees, while Gunz continued to attack. Before it was all said and done, Gunz would straddle the man and stab him more than a hundred times. Gunz stood up, holding the knife in his left hand. Blood dripped off the blade, and onto the hardwood floorboard of the bedroom.

Cassy stood up and walked over to the fallen Sanchez. She looked down on him with tears streaming down her face. She was missing Mary worse than ever. "He's finally gone. He finally reaped what he'd sown."

Gunz mugged the man's body. His heart continued to pound in his chest. "Bitch ass muthafucka wasn't nothing but a racist bully. He got what he deserved. Ain't no muthafucka finna stand in the way of my paper."

Ross slipped behind Cassy and wrapped his arm around her neck, squeezing. She slapped at his huge bicep. Her eyes bugging out of her head. "I told you, shorty, the only way out of this ma'fucka was through the Columbian, but you ain't listen." He squeezed as hard as he could.

Cassy knew it was over. She knew Ross's track record. She scratched at his hairy forearms and struggled, to no avail. In a matter of minutes, she was lifeless, and Ross was dropping her to the floor. He laid her on top of Sanchez and took a step back, admiring both bodies. "I don't know why ma'fuckas think just because a nigga got money, he ain't about that life?" He laughed. "Mane, let's get the fuck out of here."

Ghost

Chapter 16

Jock sat in his truck and waited for Marvey's daughter, Amira, to walk into the hair salon. He waited twenty minutes before he got out of his truck and followed directly behind her. He had been tracking her ever since she had left her condo only a few hours prior. Out of all of Marvey's children, Jock knew Amira was his favorite. She was his only daughter. Besides her, he had two sons that lived in Haiti with their mother. Marvey was a special kind of man. Jock knew he couldn't just run up in the man's mansion without being met with all kinds of opposition, so he figured it was in his best interest to find a way to make the man come to him, alone. That way he could annihilate him and go on with his life. It was driving him crazy to know another killer as ruthless as he was, was hunting him. He hadn't gotten a decent night's rest since he'd discovered his daughter's body and had still not had the courage to bury her. He kept her body in the basement of his home, wrapped up in the deep freezer.

It was nine o'clock in the morning and the sun was already out beaming like crazy, causing Miami to feel hot and humid. The air was as thick as a peanut butter sandwich. Jock pulled open the salon's door and a bell sounded. As soon as he stepped through it, all eyes were on him. There were two black females with their heads under dryers already, and they nearly broke their necks to see who was coming through the door. There were three other females sitting in chairs along a wall, with magazines in their hands. When the bell went off on the door, they looked toward him, smiled and then started to whisper among themselves. A heavyset female with blue and white hair walked toward him with a bottle of conditioner in her hand. "Can I help you?" she asked, looking him up and down, friendly.

Jock looked over her shoulder, almost ignoring her as he saw Amira coming out of the back of the salon, rubbing her hands together as if she were rubbing lotion into them. She had her head lowered, but when she lifted it up, they locked eyes and she froze in place, then turned around to run. "Fuck!" she yelled.

The heavyset woman looked over her shoulder at Amira as she made her way to the back door that had an exit sign hanging over it. She turned to look at Jock again, now with her eyes wide, kinda putting two and two together. "I said, can I help you, sir? This is appointment day only. We aren't doing walk-ins. Can you please just…"

Jock cocked back and punched her so hard she flew back with her arms in the air and landed under a sink, with her right leg kicking repeatedly. "It's too early for you to be runnin yo muthafuckin mouth, damn!"

Amira ran to the back door and tried with all her might to open it, but the door would not budge. It seemed as if it were locked shut, and then she remembered three weeks ago, someone kept on breaking into their salon by the back door, and Sharon had gotten it nailed shut from the inside. She turned around to face her cousin as she saw him knock Sharon off her feet and into the air, before pulling a gun out of his waistband and brandishing it at the other women in the salon.

Jock smiled after he saw Amira couldn't get out of the door. He knew he had her right where he needed her to be. He backed all the way up and locked the door to the salon and flipped the sign to closed, before pulling the blinds down. "Now, I want every last one of you bitchez to get on yo stomachs right the fuck now. Anybody that don't do what I say, I'm stanking you right away." To drive his point home, he stepped over to Sharon, put the barrel to her forehead. *Boom!* Her brains splattered against the linoleum floor. Blood ran from the back of her head and into a drain by his foot. The other females in the store screamed and began to panic with the fear of losing their lives. Jock took a step back and aimed his gun at Amira. "Bitch, get yo ass over here right now!" he hollered, walking toward her.

Amira felt like her life was over. Her father had already told her they were in a war with her cousin Jock for things he could not explain to her. His orders were for her to be smart and careful until things blew over. She didn't know what they were at odds about, but she knew both men were equally crazy, and she didn't want to be in the middle of it. She slowly walked toward Jock with her hands in front of her. "Look, Jock. I don't know what you got going on with my father, but that shit ain't got nothing to do with me. Leave me out of it, please," she whimpered, feeling her knees knocking.

Jock looked over his dark-skinned cousin and felt no sympathy for her whatsoever. Even though she was beautiful, all he saw was Marvey's face every time he looked at her. He hated the man for trying to have him killed. He hated the man for still having a daughter that was alive and Aerial was gone. He reached and grabbed Amira by the throat, before slinging her into a full-length mirror. She crashed into the mirror and it shattered loudly, before she fell on her face on the floor with shards of glass all around her. Jock came over and picked her up by the hair, placing his forehead to hers. "Bitch, you gone help me to get into position, so I can kill yo punk ass father. If you don't, after I kill every one of these bitches in this shop, I'm gon' chop yo ass up piece by piece, then I'm snatching up yo son, and trust and believe before it's all said and done, I'm gon' get that nigga. You know how I get down, so what you gon' do?" he growled, before picking her back up and throwing her into another full-length mirror, knocking her out cold.

He turned on the balls of his feet and snatched up the first female closest to him, put the pistol to her temple while she hollered and begged for him to let her live. *Boom*! Her brains shot out of her temple and landed on the woman laying on her stomach next to her. He dropped her to the ground and picked up the next chick. In his mind, all of them were Dymond. All of them where the woman that had double crossed him and killed his daughter.

To Be Continued…
A Savage Dopeboy 3
Coming Soon

Submission Guideline

Submit the first three chapters of your completed manuscript to ldpsubmissions@gmail.com, subject line: Your book's title. The manuscript must be in a .doc file and sent as an attachment. Document should be in Times New Roman, double spaced and in size 12 font. Also, provide your synopsis and full contact information. If sending multiple submissions, they must each be in a separate email.

Have a story but no way to send it electronically? You can still submit to LDP/Ca$h Presents. Send in the first three chapters, written or typed, of your completed manuscript to:

LDP: Submissions Dept
Po Box 870494
Mesquite, Tx 75187

DO NOT send original manuscript. Must be a duplicate.

Provide your synopsis and a cover letter containing your full contact information.

Thanks for considering LDP and Ca$h Presents.

BOW DOWN TO MY GANGSTA

By **Ca$h**

TORN BETWEEN TWO

By **Coffee**

THE STREETS STAINED MY SOUL **II**

By **Marcellus Allen**

BLOOD OF A BOSS **VI**

SHADOWS OF THE GAME II

By **Askari**

LOYAL TO THE GAME **IV**

By **T.J. & Jelissa**

A DOPEBOY'S PRAYER **II**

By **Eddie "Wolf" Lee**

IF LOVING YOU IS WRONG… **III**

By **Jelissa**

TRUE SAVAGE **VII**

MIDNIGHT CARTEL II

DOPE BOY MAGIC III

By **Chris Green**

BLAST FOR ME **III**

DUFFLE BAG CARTEL **IV**

A SAVAGE DOPEBOY III

By **Ghost**

A HUSTLER'S DECEIT III

KILL ZONE **II**

BAE BELONGS TO ME III

SOUL OF A MONSTER III

By **Aryanna**

THE COST OF LOYALTY **III**

By **Kweli**

CHAINED TO THE STREETS II

By **J-Blunt**

KING OF NEW YORK V

COKE KINGS IV

BORN HEARTLESS IV

By **T.J. Edwards**

GORILLAZ IN THE BAY V

De'Kari

THE STREETS ARE CALLING II

Duquie Wilson

KINGPIN KILLAZ IV

STREET KINGS III

PAID IN BLOOD III

CARTEL KILLAZ IV

Hood Rich

SINS OF A HUSTLA II

ASAD

TRIGGADALE III

Elijah R. Freeman

KINGZ OF THE GAME V

Playa Ray

SLAUGHTER GANG IV

RUTHLESS HEART II

By Willie Slaughter

THE HEART OF A SAVAGE II

By Jibril Williams

FUK SHYT II

By Blakk Diamond

THE DOPEMAN'S BODYGAURD II

By Tranay Adams

TRAP GOD II

By Troublesome

YAYO III

A SHOOTER'S AMBITION II

By S. Allen

GHOST MOB

Stilloan Robinson

KINGPIN DREAMS II

By Paper Boi Rari

CREAM

By Yolanda Moore

SON OF A DOPE FIEND II

By Renta

FOREVER GANGSTA II

By Adrian Dulan

LOYALTY AIN'T PROMISED

By Keith Williams

THE PRICE YOU PAY FOR LOVE II

By Destiny Skai

THE LIFE OF A HOOD STAR

By Rashia Wilson

TOE TAGZ II

By Ah'Million

CONFESSIONS OF A GANGSTA II

By Nicholas Lock

PAID IN KARMA II

By Meesha

I'M NOTHING WITHOUT HIS LOVE II

By Monet Dragun

CAUGHT UP IN THE LIFE II

By Robert Baptiste

Available Now

RESTRAINING ORDER **I & II**

By **CA$H & Coffee**

LOVE KNOWS NO BOUNDARIES **I II & III**

By **Coffee**

RAISED AS A GOON I, II, III & IV

BRED BY THE SLUMS I, II, III

BLAST FOR ME I & II

ROTTEN TO THE CORE I II III

A BRONX TALE I, II, III

DUFFEL BAG CARTEL I II III

HEARTLESS GOON I II III IV

A SAVAGE DOPEBOY I II

HEARTLESS GOON I II III

DRUG LORDS I II III

By **Ghost**

LAY IT DOWN **I & II**

LAST OF A DYING BREED

BLOOD STAINS OF A SHOTTA I & II III

By **Jamaica**

LOYAL TO THE GAME

LOYAL TO THE GAME II

LOYAL TO THE GAME III

LIFE OF SIN I, II III

By **TJ & Jelissa**

BLOODY COMMAS I & II

SKI MASK CARTEL I II & III

KING OF NEW YORK I II,III IV

RISE TO POWER I II III

COKE KINGS I II III

BORN HEARTLESS I II III

By **T.J. Edwards**

IF LOVING HIM IS WRONG…I & II

LOVE ME EVEN WHEN IT HURTS I II III

By **Jelissa**

WHEN THE STREETS CLAP BACK I & II III

By **Jibril Williams**

A DISTINGUISHED THUG STOLE MY HEART I II & III

LOVE SHOULDN'T HURT I II III IV

RENEGADE BOYS I II III IV

PAID IN KARMA

By **Meesha**

A GANGSTER'S CODE I &, II III

A GANGSTER'S SYN I II III

THE SAVAGE LIFE I II III

CHAINED TO THE STREETS

By J-Blunt

PUSH IT TO THE LIMIT

By **Bre' Hayes**

BLOOD OF A BOSS **I, II, III, IV, V**

SHADOWS OF THE GAME

By **Askari**

THE STREETS BLEED MURDER **I, II & III**

THE HEART OF A GANGSTA I II& III

By **Jerry Jackson**

CUM FOR ME

CUM FOR ME 2

CUM FOR ME 3

CUM FOR ME 4

CUM FOR ME 5

An **LDP Erotica Collaboration**

BRIDE OF A HUSTLA **I II & II**

THE FETTI GIRLS **I, II& III**

CORRUPTED BY A GANGSTA I, II III, IV

BLINDED BY HIS LOVE

THE PRICE YOU PAY FOR LOVE

By **Destiny Skai**

WHEN A GOOD GIRL GOES BAD

By **Adrienne**

THE COST OF LOYALTY I II

By Kweli

A GANGSTER'S REVENGE **I II III & IV**

THE BOSS MAN'S DAUGHTERS

THE BOSS MAN'S DAUGHTERS II

THE BOSSMAN'S DAUGHTERS III

THE BOSSMAN'S DAUGHTERS IV

THE BOSS MAN'S DAUGHTERS **V**

A SAVAGE LOVE **I & II**

BAE BELONGS TO ME I II

A HUSTLER'S DECEIT I, II, III

WHAT BAD BITCHES DO I, II, III

SOUL OF A MONSTER I II

KILL ZONE

By **Aryanna**

A KINGPIN'S AMBITON

A KINGPIN'S AMBITION **II**

I MURDER FOR THE DOUGH

By **Ambitious**

TRUE SAVAGE

TRUE SAVAGE II

TRUE SAVAGE **III**

TRUE SAVAGE **IV**

TRUE SAVAGE **V**

TRUE SAVAGE **VI**

DOPE BOY MAGIC I, II

MIDNIGHT CARTEL

By **Chris Green**

A DOPEBOY'S PRAYER

By **Eddie "Wolf" Lee**

THE KING CARTEL **I, II & III**

By **Frank Gresham**

THESE NIGGAS AIN'T LOYAL **I, II & III**

By **Nikki Tee**

GANGSTA SHYT **I II &III**

By **CATO**

THE ULTIMATE BETRAYAL

By **Phoenix**

BOSS'N UP **I , II & III**

By **Royal Nicole**

I LOVE YOU TO DEATH

By Destiny J

I RIDE FOR MY HITTA

I STILL RIDE FOR MY HITTA

By **Misty Holt**

LOVE & CHASIN' PAPER

By **Qay Crockett**

TO DIE IN VAIN

SINS OF A HUSTLA

By **ASAD**

BROOKLYN HUSTLAZ

By **Boogsy Morina**

BROOKLYN ON LOCK I & II

By **Sonovia**

GANGSTA CITY

By **Teddy Duke**

A DRUG KING AND HIS DIAMOND I & II III

A DOPEMAN'S RICHES

HER MAN, MINE'S TOO I, II

CASH MONEY HO'S

By Nicole Goosby

TRAPHOUSE KING **I II & III**

KINGPIN KILLAZ I II III

STREET KINGS I II

PAID IN BLOOD **I II**

CARTEL KILLAZ I II III

By **Hood Rich**

LIPSTICK KILLAH **I, II, III**

CRIME OF PASSION I II & III

By **Mimi**

STEADY MOBBN' **I, II, III**

THE STREETS STAINED MY SOUL

By **Marcellus Allen**

WHO SHOT YA **I, II, III**

SON OF A DOPE FIEND

Renta

GORILLAZ IN THE BAY **I II III IV**

DE'KARI

TRIGGADALE I II

Elijah R. Freeman
GOD BLESS THE TRAPPERS I, II, III
THESE SCANDALOUS STREETS I, II, III
FEAR MY GANGSTA I, II, III
THESE STREETS DON'T LOVE NOBODY I, II
BURY ME A G I, II, III, IV, V
A GANGSTA'S EMPIRE I, II, III, IV
THE DOPEMAN'S BODYGAURD
Tranay Adams
THE STREETS ARE CALLING
Duquie Wilson
MARRIED TO A BOSS... I II III
By Destiny Skai & Chris Green
KINGZ OF THE GAME I II III IV
Playa Ray
SLAUGHTER GANG I II III
RUTHLESS HEART
By Willie Slaughter
THE HEART OF A SAVAGE
By Jibril Williams
FUK SHYT
By Blakk Diamond
DON'T F#CK WITH MY HEART I II
By Linnea
ADDICTED TO THE DRAMA I II III
By Jamila
YAYO I II

A SHOOTER'S AMBITION

By S. Allen

TRAP GOD

By Troublesome

FOREVER GANGSTA

By Adrian Dulan

TOE TAGZ

By Ah'Million

KINGPIN DREAMS

By Paper Boi Rari

CONFESSIONS OF A GANGSTA

By Nicholas Lock

I'M NOTHING WITHOUT HIS LOVE

By Monet Dragun

CAUGHT UP IN THE LIFE

By Robert Baptiste

BOOKS BY LDP'S CEO, CA$H

TRUST IN NO MAN

TRUST IN NO MAN 2

TRUST IN NO MAN 3

BONDED BY BLOOD

SHORTY GOT A THUG

THUGS CRY

THUGS CRY 2

THUGS CRY 3

TRUST NO BITCH

TRUST NO BITCH 2

TRUST NO BITCH 3

TIL MY CASKET DROPS

RESTRAINING ORDER

RESTRAINING ORDER 2

IN LOVE WITH A CONVICT

Coming Soon

BONDED BY BLOOD 2

BOW DOWN TO MY GANGSTA

Ghost

3 1333 04987 4363

9 781951 081